STUFF I FORGOT
TO REMEMBER

STUFF I FORGOT TO REMEMBER

BERNICE ZAKIN

Copyright © 2013 by Bernice Zakin.

Library of Congress Control Number:		2013910668
ISBN:	Hardcover	978-1-4836-5385-3
	Softcover	978-1-4836-5384-6
	Ebook	978-1-4836-5386-0

All rights reserved. No part of this book may be reproduced or transmitted in any form or by any means, electronic or mechanical, including photocopying, recording, or by any information storage and retrieval system, without permission in writing from the copyright owner.

This is a work of fiction. Names, characters, places and incidents either are the product of the author's imagination or are used fictitiously, and any resemblance to any actual persons, living or dead, events, or locales is entirely coincidental.

This book was printed in the United States of America.

Rev. date: 06/27/2013

To order additional copies of this book, contact:
Xlibris Corporation
1-888-795-4274
www.Xlibris.com
Orders@Xlibris.com
128640

TABLE OF CONTENTS

Nothing In Particular But Important 11
More Stuff 13
Where I Used To Live 14
Then And Now 19
Books From My Early Childhood 21
Flickering Lights 23
My First Time Driving Alone 25
A Time To Celebrate 27
Officer It Wasn't My Fault 30
Birthday Dilemma 32
A Pretty Pickle 34
What Little Things Make Me Happy? 36
What Does This Computer Think It Is Anyway? 38
Words 40
Lucky Me 42
At Sea 45
How To Dehoard And What To Dispose Of Or Not To Buy 46
My Pecularities 49
What Shall I Do? 52
Under The Weather 56
What It Feels Like To Be 90 Or More 58
Sad To Say 61
As Time Goes On 63
She Missed The Boat 64
This Modern Age 66
Bed Solutions 68

Wonderful Me	70
My BFF	71
A Visit From Afar	72
What News Is Fit To Print?	74
How To Have Fun	76
Attention North Pole	78
When I Feel Sorry For Myself	79
Relentless Dream	80
Perchance To Dream	82
The Perfect Solution	84
Tis A Puzzlement	86
Green	87
Is Anyone Calling?	89
How Old Is "Old"	91
I Am The Cookie Monster	92
Fare Thee Well Sweet Things	94
The Sounding Board	96
Friends To The End	97
Winning Is Everything	98
A Big Event	101
Hair Today—Gone Tomorrow	103
People I've Known And Their Attributes As Well As Their Idiosyncrasies	105
I Think I'm Right	108
Packing For A Trip	110
I'm An Escalator	112
I'm Sad	114
Togetherness	117
A Letter To Someone I Hate	119
Ladies Night Out	121
Knock Knock Who's There	124
Gone Are The Dailies, etc	125
The People Who Are Out To "Get" You	127

What's White All Over?	130
A Happy Conclusion Is Just An Illusion	131
The Awkward Years	133
Amen	134
Barbi	136
September 7, 2013	138
Things You Never Knew About Nancy	140
Nancy	144
70+30 = 100 For Nancy And Jeff	146
Jeff	147
My Son Kenny	149
Lizzie Then And Now	151
Jon	153
Jon At 59—2012	154
December 7, 2013—Miami	155
Ira	157
Elaine	158
Apologies To The Red Guy At A Nearby Restaurant	160
Holiday Blues	162
Sic Sick	164
Weiner—Get Cleaner!	165
What To Do!	166
High Hopes	168
Election Selection	169
Let's Go Back	170
Attention—America	172
Older And Bolder	173
Home Sweet Home	175
Silence	177
She Was Tall, Blonde, Beautiful And Nice	178
"There's Someone On The Roof"	180
The Room Fell Quiet As The Door Opened And . . .	184
"Sew" Shall Ye Reap	187

Caroline	189
Perfect Crime	192
Who Am I?	196
Speechless In Tampa	199
"God Knows" Written Just Before The Election Returns	201
At Last It's Over	203
Who Will Be The Winner?	205
What To Do Now?	209
Tragedy And Treason	211
Pangs	213
To Whom It May Concern	214
Emailperson.Com	216
Boy Meets Girl	218
From The "Seasoning" To The "Season"	220
Who Knows?	222
Humor	224
Rumor Has It	225
Tsimmis	227
Poachers	229
How To Choose An M.D.	230
If Things Were Reversed	232
Vertigo Or Where To Go	233
Our Power	234
Not Well	236
MRI	237
The Elucidation Of A Lack Of Talent	240

DEDICATION

(A repeat from previous books but always relevant)

Always to the memory of my late husband Albert Zakin

To my children Nancy and Jeff, and Barbi and Ken

All my grandchildren: Lizzie and Jon, Carly and Peter, Andy and Dana, David and Susan, Kenny and Alyson and Debbie and Michael

Finally my great grandchildren: 13 in number and they are not to be slighted, but are too numerous to name individually

(I do know their names however!)

Nothing In Particular But Important

This entire book is the result of the collaborative efforts of the Xlibris staff who did the actual printing and handled all the technicalities of its production and publication.

And let's not forget Elise Alarimo who transcribed all of the material and conducted the business end so ably. She made the many telephone calls, filled out various forms and arranged the entire table of contents, etc and was incredibly involved throughout this entire procedure.

Also I want to thank Elaine Winik whose suggestions as to some of the titles of these essays in addition to her dedication and constant encouragement in her writing classes was so invaluable to me.

Plus Marcus—I certainly do thank you for being my ongoing ink supplier. How would I be able to write without it.

Finally, I (Bernice) designed and drew the book's front cover as I did with all 8 of my other books and of course I am totally responsible for the literary contents.

More Stuff

Well here we are again. I've written some more "stuff" because one thought seems to lead to another and boom all of a sudden I've got another whole book load.

I absolutely did not intend writing another book because very honestly it involves using a tremendous amount of paper and ink. In addition my pens dry up, to say nothing of the time that's involved, which could certainly be used for other things.

For instance I could go to the movies, I could talk to people on the telephone, and I could play more bridge, or make luncheon dates. I could even shop, especially if there is a sale someplace or possibly take a trip!

Another thing, sometimes these thoughts pop up in the middle of the night and I'm torn as to whether I should get out of bed to write them down. If I don't get up I'll be sorry in the morning because by that time I will have forgotten the entire scenario of ideas. On the other hand if I do get up it might be very difficult to fall asleep again. So my dilemma is a matter of choice. Do I get up or stay put? On a cold night I'll stay snuggly in bed, and if it is "warmer" I'll hop out of bed and start to scribble, so in a way this book consists of some very "hot stuff".

In any event I'm now stuck with all of it, so I'm obligated to have the stuff printed just to get rid of it, therefore here it is!

WHERE I USED TO LIVE

Whenever I develop a new friendship, that person is inclined to ask me where I live, and naturally I supply her with my current address. In most instances after that the question will arise as to where I lived before I lived where I presently live.

This then becomes a problem for me to explain. You see my entire lifetime has involved my moving from one place to another. Not that I am a nomad or that my family was evading the law, it is simply that a series of circumstances caused my constant uprooting, as I will now try to make clear.

My first abode was an apartment in Manhattan on West 161th Street and Riverside Drive where I lived for the first 6 years of my life. Then my family moved to 157th street in order to be closer to my grade school which was on 151st Street.

When I was 10 my family moved to 86th Street and Riverside Drive, which was a more convenient area, and in which I lived until I got married. In the interim we moved twice, once to 89th Street and West End Avenue, and finally to 87th Street and the Drive. The reason for these moves was because my mother hated having painters disrupt her household and in those years apartments were painted every 2 years. Therefore to avoid a paint job we moved to 89th Street. However my father liked living on the Drive as it was much cooler there in the days before air conditioning so that was why we ultimately moved to 87th Street 2 years later.

All went well until I got married and moved to Peoria, Illinois which was where my husband was born and where we lived in a hotel for 6 months until we were able to find a suitable apartment. Finally we found a lovely one where we lived for almost 2 years.

Sadly the Second World War broke out during that time and my husband was called up for army service. However the day before he was to leave to join his group he played football and severely injured his leg, so when he arrived at the army base they immediately put him in 4F and sent him to Rockford, Illinois to buy war materiel for the army.

We lived there in a hotel for 6 months and then he was transferred to New York City where we lived in another hotel across the street from my parent's apartment. This was a very good plan as it meant that we were able to have free meals at their home during that time.

After another year and a half, Al was transferred to Fort Worth, Texas where we lived in a hotel for 6 months and then were able to rent an adorable house where my daughter was born and we were able to live like normal people and to develop a wonderful social life.

Finally the war ended and we considered remaining in Texas where Al had been offered a wonderful opportunity to go into a new business, something called "air conditioning", however a series of frantic telephone calls from my parents, pleading with us to return to New York where they were anxious to enjoy being with their only grandchild, and where Al was offered a partnership in my father's very successful jewelry business.

Al had been in the farm machinery business in Peoria, but since that business had not resumed manufacturing after the war ended, my father's offer seemed logical even though it meant that Al would have to go to night school at Columbia for 2 years to completely learn the jewelry trade. He did this and so we moved to a rented apartment in New York City for 6 months during which time we tried to buy a house in Westchester to no avail, as nothing old was available and new construction had not yet started.

Finally after our 6 month rental in New York had expired, we were offered an apartment in Far Rockaway for another 6 months, after which we had to move again. This apartment was also in Far Rockaway, but it was a much larger one on 2 acres on the top floor of a mansion like home, where my son was born.

We stayed there for 3 years until we were able to buy a newly constructed house in Lawrence in 1951 where we stayed for 45 years.

This proved to be an extremely fortuitous move as Al and my father's business changed and expanded considerably during that time.

They opened many jewelry concessions in various resort hotels. This included the Palm Beach Hotel, The Grand

Hotel in Highmount, New York, The Laurel in the Pines in Lakewood, NJ, The Nautilus in Atlantic Beach, The Hollywood Hotel in Hollywood, Florida, The Doral Beach Hotel in Miami and The Breakers in Palm Beach, plus the Lido in Long Beach.

During those years in Palm Beach, we lived in 3 houses for 6 month periods in the Winter on Miraflores Drive, Seminole Ave and Park Ave.

In Hollywood, Florida we lived at the hotel and at the Doral we also lived at the hotel.

Since these hotels with the exception of the Doral were only open during the winter months my children were uprooted quite a bit. They never saw snow and constantly had to make new friends—not the greatest way of life—to be sure.

To further complete my moving history (you see I'm not through moving yet); I must explain that my father passed away on New Years Day at the Palm Beach Hotel in 1954 which meant that my husband had to maintain the jewelry business alone with the exception of having very able employees with him in the various Florida Hotel shops.

In 1986 he gave up the hotel concessions and just kept his New York office, thereby enabling us to go to Arizona during the next 18 winters where we used to supply jewelry to various shops in Scottsdale and where we both played lots of golf, had the most enjoyable vacations and met the greatest people. We also rented 5 different houses during the years we lived there.

By this time you must be in total disbelief as to my roving lifestyle, but I must say it was absolutely wonderful. We met and became friends with terrific people from all over the country and to this day I am fortunately able to maintain many of these friendships.

For the past 14 years I have lived on Long Island, NY at the North Shore Towers during the summer months, which I enjoy tremendously but of course I still consider Palm Beach my second home. Incidentally, I lived in 2 different apartments at the North Shore Towers during those 14 summers.

In any event I presume that it is understandable when I say it is so difficult to enumerate my various domiciles—but you must admit that it is a very "moving" story!

P.S. I forgot to mention that I've been back in Palm Beach for the past 7 winters, but in the same apartment.

Then And Now

When I was a little girl about 9 or 10 years of age, I was privileged to live in an apartment house on West 86th Street in New York City right opposite the building where William Randolph Hearst owned the top 4 floors.

His 4th floor was a ballroom and he usually had very festive parties with many celebrities in attendance, and which required the use of that room.

I must confess that I as a snoopy type of youngster (who owned a pair of binoculars) spent many an evening avidly watching the arrival of Mr. Hearst's glamorous guests, at which time he customarily laid out a plush red carpet, from the lobby of the building to the gutter, so no guest would have to tread on the sidewalk.

Also these fancy people generally arrived in extremely formal attire, with the ladies garbed in floor length ermine coats which necessitated the protection of the carpet.

Since I lived up high enough in my building, I was able to peer very closely into the Hearst ballroom, and therefore I happily glimpsed these elegant guests dancing merrily away to the most popular tunes of the day.

You might say that I was able to see "the upstairs and the downstairs" extremely well, although that television show did not exist in those years.

At any rate, my childhood nosiness differed greatly from the views I now have from my present dwelling.

Today when I peer at the building opposite me, (also with my new binoculars) I witness entirely different happenings.

I usually see an elderly couple having breakfast on their terrace, or a lady watering her plants from another terrace, and occasionally a bare topped gentleman basking in the sun.

I can assure you that what I see today is not as glamorous as what I previously saw during my preteen days, but on the other hand if my current neighbors were to peer at me now on my terrace, no doubt they would not do so with the same excitement I felt in my childhood.

Actually what they'd most probably see is a not so young, fairly unkempt person, casually attired in an unattractive cotton housecoat, very much in need of a shower.

Books From My Early Childhood

"My name is Dickey Dare" was the first line in the very first book I remember reading when I started grade school.

After that, it was like a river opened, swelled and flowed constantly, because I never stopped reading.

"A Child's Garden of Verses" was my introduction to poetry and as a second grade assignment I wrote my own little verse which I still remember

There was an old man from Kerplunk
Who took a drink and got drunk
He was reading the news
And walked out of his shoes
That crazy old man of Kerplunk

My reading matter continued with "Little Black Sambo", The "Prudence Parlin" series, "Honey Bunch and her sister Sue". "The Bobbsey Twins" and several mysteries, the names of which I don't recall, however they were all written by Augusta Hewell Seaman.

Then came the "Nancy Drew" books, "The Little Prince" "Grimms Fairy tales" and so many others.

On my ninth birthday I received a copy of "the Count of Monte Cristo" which I still own and have read at least 3 or 4 times. "Little Women" was followed by "Little Men", Huckleberry Finn", "Now We Are Six" as well as the other "Pooh and Christopher Robin" books which were all favorites on my book shelves.

And since I was often afflicted with various childhood diseases, I spent a great deal of time in bed reading the 20 volumes of the "Book of Knowledge" which I really adored and as a result I thoroughly enjoyed being ill as well.

That series, plus my mother's rice pudding, custards and hot beef tea made staying in bed delightful experiences in my childhood.

To sum it up I don't believe I have ever gone a day since then without opening a book and hopefully I never shall.

FLICKERING LIGHTS

I guess I had been married about 6 months, and was certainly not particularly adept in preparing very edible items kitchen wise. In fact, to the contrary I was absolutely unable to prepare any food of a tasteworthy nature.

Unfortunately my new husband had high hopes that he hadn't bought "a pig in a poke" in choosing me as his wife. As a result one day he informed me that it was his turn to invite his fraternity brothers to our apartment for dinner. He never doubted my culinary abilities, and I had exactly 3 days before the group would arrive.

Apparently one of the young men was bringing his mother's famous strudel for dessert and I could easily manage hors d'oeuvres but what then? What could I possibly serve next?

Al assured me that it could be very simple. Maybe just salad, hamburgers and baked potatoes.

I consulted the various cook books I had newly acquired and decided it might be possible for me to make this evening a success.

All went well during the cocktail hour. I did not take part in this part of the activities as apparently the ritual did not allow the presence of wives, nor females in general to be included. All I had to do was say "hello" and "welcome", then cook and clean up.

However shortly after my ill shaped hamburgers went in the oven, the lights began to flicker and I could not imagine what was happening until the electricity went off completely. Disaster—disaster—what to do? Actually I didn't do anything. After a harrowing one half hour, one of the young men came to my rescue. He put a copper penny into the fuse box and voila! The lights went on again.

Later on I found out that such an illegal maneuver could possibly cause a fire but thankfully no such calamity occurred.

The half baked dinner survived, the strudel was a rousing success and everybody went home hoping never to visit us again.

Then because I had worked so hard and was under such a strain, my husband suggested that I leave the soiled dishes until the next morning.

That was the mistake of the century! Never to be repeated! Have you ever tried to remove 12 hour dried mustard from dishes prior to the ownership of dish washing machines? Impossible!

It took several hours the next day to clean that kitchen and I never made hamburgers again. In fact, I myself never tasted one.

My First Time Driving Alone

When I first lived in Palm Beach, I did not know how to drive,

Oh yes we owned a car—a nice shiny bright blue Buick, which was much admired by half the town. This was in the early postwar years when new cars were at a premium, and as my husband's brother was a Buick dealer in Peoria, Illinois, we were fortunate enough to get one of the first "hot off the assembly line" vehicles.

However, no matter how lovely the car was, it was still necessary for me to learn how to drive it, in order to fully appreciate its usefulness.

Jerry Connelly, a former police officer who at that time was employed as a guard at my husband's jewelry shop, made a kind offer to teach me the basics of manipulating an auto.

So the two of us soon spent many afternoons cruising around North County Road, and in and out of side streets from the ocean to the intercoastal.

After paying a modicum of attention to Jerry's invaluable instructions, I finally learned to drive ahead, back up, stop when necessary, and even to park diagonally.

Backing into a parking space however was not one of my achievements. But I didn't have to worry about that because in those days Worth Avenue only had diagonal parking and lucky me, I never went to West Palm.

Soon the challenging day arrived when I had to take my driving test in order to get a license (that magical card that would entitle me to be a real person in the eyes of the driving world).

Unfortunately this test had to take place in West Palm where I had to really park properly.

"Don't despair" Jerry said, "I can guarantee that you will pass the test, and the license will be yours".

At that point he explained how he was so positive this would happen. In a very knowledgeable manner Jerry said "just put a $5.00 bill on the seat next to you during the test and the license will be in the mail".

He certainly was right and I got my license. Some years later I learned to back into a parking space correctly.

Nevertheless in addition to getting my license I really learned an invaluable financial lesson"!

A Time To Celebrate

June 29th—a memorable day—I would have been married 71 years if only my husband had lived to enjoy it. We were lucky enough however to celebrate 67 years together.

Nevertheless this is still a time for enjoyment as I am presently sitting in a nice green wicker chair on a country porch high in the hills of Vermont, at a place called "Twin Farms".

I am here with 4 grandchildren and their spouses, plus my daughter Nancy and her husband Jeff on the eventful occasion of his 70th birthday and their 30th wedding anniversary.

Luckily we arrived here today and were just in time for a wonderful lunch. This included a tasty lobster salad on a home baked roll, hot vegetable soup served in a lovely vee shaped glass, fresh grown greens artfully arranged on top of young asparagus and yellow squash—all from the Twins Farms' very ample garden.

The dessert was decorative indeed. It was lemon curd on top of a home baked cookie topped with fresh blackberries and whipped cream; there were 2 extensions from the cookie (one on each side) of toasted meringue on top of more whipped cream. It was all extremely attractive and utterly delicious.

The place itself is wondrous. The main house, in which I am staying, dates back to 1794 and has a myriad amount of rooms completely filled with yesteryears antiques and bibelots. Everything is artistically and cozily placed and denotes comfort and a feeling of going back in time.

One of the gentlemen in charge of the farm told me that Sinclair Lewis used to stay here and that in fact this was where he wrote "Babbitt". My room, which is called the Washington Room has all the walls filled with engravings of President Washington as well as many 18th century items relating to early Americana, even a copy of Washington's inaugural speech.

There is absolutely everything here to make a guest feel comfortable and entertained, even a little gift package containing a small jigsaw puzzle.

The large living room has a scrabble board, a checker set, several book shelves filled with enticing volumes and many seating areas which are comfortable indeed. It is not possible to spend an idle moment if you do not so desire.

My children and grandchildren are all staying in another part of the farm and each little area is equally quaint and inviting.

I'm so happy that I am able to be here and to hear the birds sing sweet little melodies and to listen to their happy chirping.

Also I am presently looking around at all the tall trees, which are dipping down from a mountainous high hill to a sloping sun filled valley. There are pretty pink flowers tucked between old stones and logs, and although everything in front of me is magnificent, I can only imagine how delightful it must be here in the winter time when there is snow on the ground as well as cake like frosting on the tree tops. They have postcards here indicating that this is so.

Right now as luck would have it the sun is shining and the sky is blue and I can even see a very faint shadow of a distant mountain in the sky and a tiny tuft of a white cloud. Breathing in the fresh air is like opening an expensive bottle of perfume and inhaling. What can possibly be more pleasurable?

We all expect to be here for 4 days and I know they will be wonderful. I also believe that on our final evening, there will be many poems and speeches, that I and my grandchildren will make in order to pay tribute to Nancy and Jeff on these two equally great occasions.

I am truly grateful to Jeff for arranging such an unusual way for our family to celebrate together, and can only hope we may continue to do so again in the years to come.

Officer It Wasn't My Fault

I am a very careful driver—in fact probably too careful. I slow down at yellow lights. I give signals at all times. I stay in my lane usually on the right side of the road, and I am never in a hurry. Let the wild ones speed ahead. It doesn't matter to me.

However, I *once* got a ticket. My only one, and that was years ago.

I was enroute to the Lido Hotel in Long Beach around 6PM on a Saturday night in the summertime so that I could have dinner with my husband who had a jewelry shop there.

As I was proceeding along in my usual careful fashion, the car in front of me suddenly stopped short and my car tapped his car very slightly, then the car behind me rammed into my car.

So there I was sandwiched between two vehicles and innocent as a newborn lamb. My car was not damaged nor were the other two cars. However the man in the front car immediately called the police and yelled "oh my aching back"! I knew he couldn't possibly be hurt but it didn't matter to the policeman who arrived on the scene, even though I proclaimed that it certainly was not my fault and even though I also said that nobody's car was damaged in the slightest way. Nevertheless the man in front kept claiming an injury.

Naturally I got a ticket because I was glamorously attired in evening clothes and looked like I was "out on the town" and not to be trusted driving wise.

Several years later at the Woodmere Club, my husband and I were introduced to an attorney, and when he heard our name he said smugly "I remember you. I once got a client of mine $12,000 on a claim he made against you in Atlantic Beach". I responded irritably "But he wasn't even hurt". The attorney gleefully answered "of course not, I know he wasn't hurt but I'm a good attorney"!

BIRTHDAY DILEMMA

I recently had a birthday and yes it was celebrated merrily, lavishly and with many friends and family members present to cheer me on to my next set of years.

I had also thoroughly specified on my invitations that I did not desire any gifts. However several of my guests ignored this request and either brought or sent me lovely items which I must admit I am now every happy to own.

It was also apparent that 5 ingenious people huddled together and made the decision to plop down a goodly sum to purchase a very handsome and expensive purse as a shared gift for me. The purse is truly lovely, very useful and naturally requires my heartfelt thank yous!

But now this is my problem. How do I do this—do I thank each person for a particular portion of this gift? How do I know who sent what? Do I thank one person for the handle? Another for the upper portion? And then one for the bottom? (It is two toned).

However that leaves the last person without any portion of the bag for which I can say thank you, or does the packaging count or did someone just pay for the delivery.

The thing is I don't really know the truth—therefore I am in much of a quandary.

I would normally write individual notes, although a recent batch of new stationary I ordered arrived with the incorrect spelling of my name so I decided to place personal calls instead.

But—what to say? Does it sound peculiar if I say thank you for the terrific handle? Or the lining is great, thanks ever so much, or how clever of you to wrap that box so excitingly, or even "I really loved the delivery man".

I honestly didn't know how to solve this problem therefore I finally resolved never to have anymore parties.

A Pretty Pickle

I must begin this article by stating a very well known fact. Almost everyone whom I list amongst my closest companions, friends and relatives, etc are aware of my love for sour pickles.

I practically have a fetish about them, indeed a daily desire for them, and certainly I admit to indulging my yearning with an everyday pickle intake.

However I have recently encountered an obstacle to this indulgence and this is the situation that has caused my dilemma.

I've purchased a strange jar of pickles! They float! They are encased in a jar of liquid and are all bunched together at the top of the jar and absolutely do not touch the bottom.

They rise above the liquid like a group of aliens in the sky and I'm unsure as to their actual physical structure. Are they human or are they possibly an alien form of cucumber? Why do they try to reach the top of the jar? What is wrong with my pickles, or maybe with my jar? Do they have *sub*human qualities? (It can't be "sub") because they are so high up.

Is their juice something like the Dead Sea? Is it the salty brine? I would really like to know because I would hate to think they descend from a human type of species, as I eat them all the time and I am *not* a kin to a carnivore.

If there is anyone out there who is knowledgeable about flying pickles, please e-mail me at your earliest convenience. *BerniceZakin@aol.com*

Thank You

What Little Things Make Me Happy?

Not only is there one little thing that makes me happy there are actually several items that do and I will be most happy to enumerate them.

1. *Pickles*—I love the ones that are half sour and slightly Jewish. They truly give me intense delight and I positively drool whenever I contemplate their deliciousness, which can be found in their bumpy little texture, their yellowish, greenish coloring and most definitely in their crunchy taste.
2. *Pasta with clam sauce*—I am filled with salivation at the very thought of this combination, especially when it is hot, hot, hot and the clam aroma permeates my nostrils. Now there are not many places where this combo can be properly obtained, particularly where a person can be *assured* of acquiring a successfully prepared and appetizing plateful of the stuff. Therefore I mostly have to cook it myself which I am proud to say I do in a very satisfactory manner. Yum Yum.
3. *Attending a sad movie or reading an equally sorrowful book*. Both of these things make me joyful, unusual as that sounds. You see they cause my eyes to overflow with mournful tears that generally fall down my

cheeks in big drips. This actually cleanses my eyes which then become brighter and enables my vision to grow sharper.

This may be a strange way of becoming happy, but since I rarely cry on unpleasant occasions, I find that weeping serves as a wonderful sensory experience, that improves my eyesight and gives me lachrymose satisfaction!

4. *Walking into a perfectly tidy room* as I love to see everything in its place, and of course I am equally content to have a place for everything.
5. *Spending time with my cute little great grandchildren* and kissing their chubby little cheeks, which is an extreme delight. Believe it or not their soggy diapers do not dismay me as they simply "whet" my appetite for the little critters—hee hee!
6. *Best of All A Rainy Day*. A bowl of soup and not having anything special to do is a most wonderful experience. The entire above listing is probably because I am essentially a lazy person with a good appetite which definitely makes me very happy!

What Does This Computer Think It Is Anyway?

I have a serious complaint to register against my computer. I do believe it hates me or at the very least it tries to rule my life and believes it thinks it's my mother.

The reason I am convinced of this is because it keeps printing news flashes like "Bernice your black ink is running low" or Bernice you need a cleanup" or Bernice if you don't do "so and so" you will get a virus, etc. Besides which I didn't even know we were on a first name basis.

Then too, it is always playing tricks on me, such as when I'm searching for a lost item and it tells me to look in various "other places". What is this? A game of "hide and seek"?

Or else the screen will suddenly go dark and the entire face of the computer will disappear which means I have to go through the whole process of rebooting.

Also it has a daily tendency of printing pop-ups (which covers my e-mail), to encourage my making purchases of things I do not need.

Now I don't know of anybody who has a solution to this problem, but if *such* a person exists I'd appreciate any information as to how I can control such arrogance.

Doesn't this computer know that it is only a machine and that I am a *real* person who deserves a modicum of respect?

Please reply ASAP! Preferably in letter form.

Words

Words, words, so many words—why are some long and why are some of them short? Why are they part of sentences, paragraphs, or in books, and dictionaries, and why are they frequently loud? Soft? Bad? Nice? Pretty? Or pretty ugly?

What do they actually mean or are they meant to be "mean", and why does the word "mean" sometimes mean "mean" 'and which of the two words "mean" come first and who decided to differentiate between them?

Also why do we sing them or whisper them? And do they merely roll off our tongues? Come out of our mouths, or are they just in our heads or only in our thoughts. If so who invented them?

Who put them in different languages? Who put them on ancient walls, on ancient shrines or on ancient tablets? Or even on modern tablets such as IPads or computer screens?

Was there really a Moses? If so did he write the words of the commandments himself? And in what language?

Why do so many words mean the same thing? And why do so many of them mean just the opposite?

Could we possibly live without them? Also why do some people say "no rhyme or reason" and where did "rhyme" itself first evolve? Was there a "reason" or did words just rhyme by accident?

Do you know the answer to all these questions. Do you know anyone who does?

I definitely don't—In fact I'm now at a loss for words!

Lucky Me

I'm about to become invincible. Nothing will ever harm me. I am going to be amazingly healthy and never have any problems.

Do you want to know how I'll be able to achieve these capabilities? I'll tell you how—I now listen to my television commercials on a daily basis and adhere faithfully to all their sales pitches.

Because of this system I'm going to reach my outstanding financial goals with "Fidelity.Gov" so I'll no longer have any money worries.

Next I'm going to buy a "Subaru' to get me where I have to go quickly and easily.

I'm also going to e-mail "Angie's List" to acquire the most qualified people in their various fields to help me in all phases of *my* life.

Then I'm going on "E-Harmony.com" to meet the man of my dreams. He will certainly be of help whenever I realize that I can't do everything myself.

I intend to take extra precautions driving on highways and will avoid walking over potholes in the street. The "Travelers

Insurance Co" will assure that I'm completely covered in case of any auto accidents or damages to my person.

Of course I'm going to vote for "Mitt Romney". He promised to bring prosperity to the nation and develop a strong economy, increase jobs, lower gas prices, etc. This means that I will be able to maintain my harmonious and prosperous lifestyle.

Also by purchasing lovely jewelry on "QVC", I'll enjoy high fashion and always look my dazzling best. "HSN" is also a possibility for my achieving the same *effects*. These items may be returned—no questions asked, if I'm dissatisfied with them.

In addition, I get my daily B vitamins in "Splenda Paks" which is an advantage when I add it to my beverages.

Do you have protection against identity theft? Well I do. I have "Lifelock" so all my sensitive documents are well taken care of in case they are stolen. Isn't that terrific?

"Veggie V8" has half the calories of other veggie juices so it certainly wins my vote! It helps to keep me in shape and really tastes great. Besides it comes in all sizes.

And did you ever have a fear of falling? Not me—because I have "Medical Alert". All I have to do is push the little button on their gizmo if by chance I do fall or need medical assistance, in that case this company will send help to me immediately.

Plus my local "CVS" has saved me hundreds of dollars, and their products keep me healthy at all times. So that's why I go there for all my medications. If I'm unable to pick up my meds I call "Med 4 homes" who will deliver them promptly.

In fact, I have every conceivable aid to keep me going. By the way "Philips Magnesia" is good for that too.

Thankfully I still have all my teeth but I can tell you most assuredly that if the occasion ever arises I will certainly keep an ample supply of "Fixadent" on hand.

To sum it all up, by listening to every ad on TV I am well equipped to survive until the next century, that is if my money lasts but if that is a problem, I can call on "Charles Schwab". I can always talk to Chuck and he will listen!

At Sea

"At Sea"—exactly what does that mean? Is it describing a moment aboard ship admiring the sleek lines of an enormous luxury liner, with the gang plank awaiting a throng of would be voyagers to ascend, and later seeing those people wave frantically at friends or relatives on the pier who are heartily wishing them a Bon Voyage.

Or perhaps for a person to lean over the ship's rail and to breathe in the tangy salt air, watching the white capped frothy blue water, with the wake trailing behind and feeling the repetitive rolling motion below? And certainly to be looking forward to a wondrous vacation.

Now this might possibly be two versions of "At Sea", however it is not mine, simply because I've never been on a cruise, and certainly have not boarded a big ship.

Therefore I prefer to think that "At Sea" simply means being completely muddled and unable to reach a conclusion to a specific problem.

Which is precisely my current dilemma!

How To Dehoard And What To Dispose Of Or Not To Buy

A great problem now exists in the lives of many people including myself.

A lot of us are inundated with "things". Now "things" can consist of several categories; articles of clothing, food stuffs, memorabilia, automotive equipment, written material and outdated electronic items.

Also people who reside in actual houses containing attics and basements are more apt to collect "things"

And those of us who live in apartments, or even just shared dwellings can often use the private storage facilities (that are now quite prevalent) to store belongings not required for everyday use.

Parting with "things" in general is sometimes like giving up a favorite member of your family, an unforgettable old boy or girl friend, or other significant memories of childhood, teen ages, adult or middle ages or maybe even a yesterdays object.

Nevertheless the time does come when shame and embarrassment justifies the decision to unload. Scrapbooks, old pictures, corsages and letters, etc come under the heading of this type of item.

When it comes to the contents of grocery cabinets, and if outdated cans and bottles come under scrutiny, (especially those with leaks and popping tops) then no wavering or hesitation should occur. Throw them out! Yes! Even though these items may still be usable or tasty, bad things could possibly happen to you physically, so better safe than sorry. I.e. put them in the garbage!

Clothing is another matter entirely. For instance if you used to wear a size 6 or 8 and the gorgeous dresses you wore to terrific social affairs or maybe special occasions with special people and you are now a size 12, 14 or (other) then those days are gone forever. They will never fit, you will never lose weight, and you might as well get rid of these fabulous doodads.

As for your original radio that had tubes, your TV that was black and white and thick, plus the portable telephone you originally bought for emergency use only, is now a non-functioning article that has no use whatsoever, so my advice is—dump them!

Now comes the most difficult decision "what not to buy".

When you pass a store window that displays beautiful items, whether it be clothing, food, jewelry or just pretty things, don't go in the store. Stores are dangerous. They try to sell things and if you crave an item they have, you might probably buy it and then you *own* it!

Also when TV channels advertise great items whether it be for the kitchen, bedroom or just clothing items, don't send for them. Again if you send for them you will *own* them and have to *pay* for them. Turn off the TV and read a book instead.

If you follow my advice you will have cleaner closets, more room for the things you really need and will also have the money you saved from not making a purchase. Isn't that nice?

(P.S. I just saw the most adorable bag on QVC and I think I have to have it—oh well!)

My Peculiarities

I confess! I have peculiarities—I do odd things and there are even odder things that I don't do.

I could easily make a list of these strange things but that would be too concise! I'd much rather be more abandoned in my explanations of them and let my readers judge me for themselves. That is If they judge me at all (and if I have any readers).

Mind you—my unusual habits may seem very normal to many people (especially to me) but alas, to a great many others, what I do or like, or dislike may appear to be quite weird.

For instance I have a fixation about pickles (half sour). I adore them and actually consume a few at each meal other than breakfast.

My other food preferences—or rather my non preferences are hamburgers (I've never had one), Ketchup (I never tasted it) white meat chicken chow mein (without the chicken), I like the flavor of the chicken but not the fowl itself (I think it's foul).

I don't eat meat other than an occasional Hot Dog hor d'oeuvre, or sometimes a steak from Peter Luger's restaurant.

I am a soup maniac and consume it twice daily.

Another one of my habits is that I am a compulsive saver. I have in my possession everything I ever owned and then some. I am therefore truly overloaded with "stuff".

I am also extremely neat—overly so—my dresser drawers and closet items are color coordinated and my shelving piles are in tidy aligned arrangements, and I don't wear new items until they are at least one or two years old.

I'm also a compulsive purchaser which is why I own so many things.

In addition I like almost everybody which most people consider to be an uncommon attribute, but I am of the opinion that most people are pleasant, nice and fun to know.

I am also particularly dedicated to specific dining habits—breakfast at 7 AM, lunch at 11:00 Am and dinner generally at 5 PM, unless by chance I have a dinner engagement with friends and then I am stuck and have to be accommodating as to their dining hour preferences. (I am definitely amiable).

Then too I remember everyone from forever but they don't remember me at all which is sad and embarrassing. I can't help another facet of my nature but I also vividly recall incidents about these people from long ago, of which they have no recollection whatsoever about these same events.

Additionally once my bed is made I will never sit on it and I fluff up chair or sofa cushions as soon as I get up from sitting. I also sneakily rearrange table ornaments if a housekeeper ever moves them so much as an inch.

Are you ever late for an appointment? Not me! I'm always very early and find myself waiting endlessly for latecomers and it doesn't bother me at all.

Also my tendency for the most part is to buy in bulk for household items and therefore I own enough toilet tissue, Kleenex, paper towels etc to supply the neighborhood which is why Costco loves me and my excess purchases have to be stored under and behind my sofas and bed—(I'm willing to share however).

All in all I admit to these oddities but I do mean well.

In any event, if any of you think you'd enjoy being my friend despite my strange habits, then call me—my telephone number is 561-659-3614 (I'm usually home eating pickles or straightening chair cushions).

WHAT SHALL I DO?

I've got a problem. A really big problem. It's so big I don't know how to solve it. You see, I am a collector, a hoarder, an accumulator, an amasser, and a storer.

Now sometimes you hear about people who have leaks or other forms of liquid overflowing in their homes, but plumbers or other fixer uppers can readily solve these difficulties.

I on the other had do not seem to have a solution for my dilemma, which is not liquid and therefore no plumber can possibly help.

Sadly, in my case I am completely swamped with unnecessary memorabilia and clothing.

Unfortunately there is absolutely no room whatsoever for any additional item in my apartment. I can never admire anything I see in a department store, specialty shop, magazine or newspaper whether it be an article of clothing, an artifact or even a book, for fear that I might be tempted to make a purchase.

Mind you, my existing items are not necessarily very old, nor even scarcely worn or recently acquired. In fact most of them are indeed quite aged, but neverthelesss they all contain poignant memories that are very dear to me.

As for instance, I presently have in my possession a notebook containing the first poems I wrote from age 7 through 10. I also have scrapbooks with pressed corsages from former boyfriends (long deceased), congratulatory telegrams (remember those?) that I received on many noteworthy occasions, scholastic commendation cards from grade school (I was smart then), letters from my husband (before we were married), letters from my mother (after my marriage) containing housewifely information, as well as a diagram in one letter which indicated how I was to place a raw roast beef in a roasting pan (it worked!)

There are also loose bank coin wrappers, several tape measures (I was a decorator), special thingamajigs to enable a clumsy person to attach buttons to various garments, hundreds of loose buttons to be attached by needle and thread to old garments in need of such buttons, and even an antique buttonhook which has existed from my childhood when high button shoes were the norm.

My collections also include many coins from various European countries, that are no longer valid since the arrival of the Euro, a tremendous cache of imitation (but fashionable) jewelry, at least 20 watches (also imitation), several *unopened* (and beautifully wrapped) gift packages (contents unknown) to give to friends just in case an appropriate occasion arises. Handbags in every hue and color (many of them) which were purchased on my first few trips to Europe, as well as recent acquisitions of new wallets of every size, a collection of flashlights for every room in the house, rubber bands also for every room of the house (these are useful on an every day basis, especially for keeping sweater sleeves elevated to the proper length of the arm).

I have approximately 15 packages of new knee high hose as I am fearful of running out of my supply and believe it or not, there are also several pairs of brand new real silk stockings from at least 25 years back (pre war? *no* post war).

There is a dresser drawer full of underwear and nightgowns, heel cushions for loose shoes of which I have at least 100 pairs, an old sable collar (how can I dispose of such an expensive item), playing cards of various types (big print, canasta, double decks, and bridge, approximately 100 decks). I won't mention the number of books I own; suffice it to say that they occupy many shelves in my bedroom, living room, den, kitchen and foyer (I'm not interested in owning a Kindle).

My photographs number in the thousands (thankfully most of them are in albums but sadly many are loose). These include photos belonging to my deceased parents and sister as well as my own. Bric a brac exists including many things that were wedding gifts to my parents (they were married in 1908) and no doubt they have increased in value lo these many years! (I hope).

Attractive scrap pads purchased on a whim, stationary from former addresses, sweaters in every shape, form and color (too many to enumerate), all kinds of cosmetics (many of which arrived in gift bags from various organizations or were included in my purchases of powder or cologne) from department stores. Probably 60 or more! Lipsticks of which 10 or so are the color most appropriate for me (But still . . . .).

I have fancy soaps and shower caps from hotels around the world, which they thoughtfully supplied to their guests, as well as the ordinary bars of soap I use daily (at least 2 dozen bars), toothpaste and tooth brushes for at least the next 3 years, and perhaps there are about 15 new combs and 10 hair brushes including electrical equipment to straighten and style ornery hairdos.

In case of burns, scratches, bruises, and cuts, I have band-aids in every size. They no doubt will be capable of covering contingencies forever.

Did I mention that I own about 50 pens purchased from Costco, which I certainly use frequently, due to my ongoing writing on the yellow pads which I also bought at Costco in packs of one dozen (these are really a bargain).

Needless to say I could go on to describe my innumerable kitchen gadgets, grocery, dish and linen closet contents but I am so ashamed at this point that I believe I will have to stop counting anything else.

I just want to say that if you or any of your friends need any item at all, I most likely own it and am willing to share!

Under The Weather

I've been a sick person—in fact a very sick person—the ailments to which I've been afflicted have been mostly respiratory—although certain side affects have been present from time to time.

This situation has come about quite recently—actually 2 weeks ago when I was happy to be the hostess at my birthday party at which 50 guests attended and all wished me well. Most of them remarked that my appearance was as they put it "terrific" so who was I to presume that ill health was in the offing. In fact, the very next day.

That next day which was a Saturday several people called to thank me for affording them a pleasant time at my party. However, I was unable to respond to them vocally because I had no voice—in fact, for the next 3 days I was unable to utter a syllable. Now many of my relations would probably be gleeful that this condition had occurred because as children are apt to do, they sometimes wish their parents would "shut up". But because I consider myself to be such a superior mother, grandmother and great grandmother, I hardly thought this was possible.

At any rate, my condition worsened and I was then beset by a sore throat, much coughing, sneezing, ennui, a possible hipitis, kneeitis and maybe toeitis—but especially laryngitis.

After that series of ailments ensued many sympathetic friends called in regards to my health. One of them said "did you see the Doctor?". I said "yes and he seemed to be fine". She laughed so I don't think that was the response she expected.

I'm now being treated medically and am also drinking many liquids on a very frequent basis so I'm also quite thankful for having indoor plumbing.

Presumably, I'm in the recovery stage so if you are either reading or hearing of this article, that is probably true and therefore I hope you are happy for me.

What It Feels Like To Be 90 Or More

If you are a person lucky enough to have finally reached the age of 90, many things can happen. For instance you may start to reminisce a great deal, especially about the things that "used to be" and believe me these items are really extremely numerous.

Furthermore not many people exist who can refute your statements, therefore this entitles you to be very smug and believable.

In this regard, perhaps you can even prevaricate a bit and pretend to remember some things that never happened (which are really big fat lies), but by mentioning them you suddenly sound very knowledgeable, which might give you an additional pleasant feeling.

Another thing about reaching this age is that you have no doubt encountered many "funny" people. I don't necessarily mean "humorous" I mean odd, unusual, strange, and peculiar, etc. As a result of this, and also because you do not put yourself in any of the categories mentioned above, you may then develop a feeling of superiority which again is quite pleasurable.

You also might become cognizant of many current happenings, such as the obituary notices that are listed in the newspapers.

More and more of these notices contain news of the passing of a lot of "almosts", you know, "almost 90" maybe 86, 87, or 89 but not quite 90. In this case you may experience the glow of having overcome the hurdle of being in the "almost" group and realize that *you* personally have actually arrived into the 90 years of age bunch—Wow!

Naturally though, it is possible that at this time you may encounter a coterie of people who utter derogatory inferences when they find out that you are 90 or over.

They may whisper among themselves 90? And still alive? Some may be jealous or dubious, and some may just be nosy and incredulous. They will say to your slightly wrinkled face and neck "my you don't look it", or "how does it feel" or "how many in your family have ever lived so long?"

You don't have to answer. You can ignore these remarks with just a smile (after all Mona Lisa is old too). You are not obligated to tell these folks what hurts you, or that you spend a lot of time going to doctors or even what pills you take. It is really none of their g.d. business, and if they are lucky enough to ever reach 90 themselves, they will find out the truth anyway (whatever that truth is).

Naturally at the juncture of being 90 the goal is to reach 100, which is the "magic number" then you get to have your name and photograph on a jelly jar and you might be mentioned on Channel 4 by Willard Scott if by chance *he* is still alive.

In this case you become a celebrity for a short time until the "almosts" I mentioned previously reach 100 also.

At times too you will undoubtedly hear about people who query "do you know how old she is? Or "guess how old she is" or you'll *never* guess how old she is", or even "if I knew how old she was I would have been nicer to her"!

Incidentally I know a man who is 103 and has "all his marbles" (as they say) and still plays bridge although he does use a cane (not to bid though) and people continually ask him "George how old are you now?"

This poor man is constantly besieged with questions about his age and he's dying to be left alone but in fact no one will leave him alone until he *is* dying.

Finally they say that the one good thing about being over 90 is that your conversational topics become most interesting. You can relate unusual happenings from yesteryear with authority and will be believed unless what you say is absolutely outrageous, such as being a survivor of the titanic sinking or that you went to school with Abraham Lincoln.

In any event it is not necessary to reveal your true age until you have reached *100*—so Happy Birthday until then!

Sad To Say

I just spent one of the saddest days of my life so far, and this is how it began.

I was on a brief respite from Florida and arrived at my apartment on Long Island where I came in contact with several of my old neighbors (I do mean old) who no longer spend their winters in Florida due to travel difficulties, and seem to be content accompanied by their walkers and in their wheelchairs.

I also visited an old friend who never leaves her apartment and sits lonesomely on her living room sofa with the TV playing (without any sound). She barely glimpses anything on it, and of course hears nothing.

This lady used to be vibrant, intelligent, most attractive and an up and about person. Now unfortunately she is conversationally in and out of the past and present.

Luckily she has round the clock help to tend to her physical needs but her children seldom visit and in general she is alone. We spent approximately 2 hours together during which time she continually lamented the fact that her 2 children (daughters) rarely came to see her, even though they call her daily.

As she put it "I don't need a voice I'd rather have a body". It seems that these children are usually away on pleasure trips, and I guess that they also find that visiting their mother represents an unpleasant task, and I presume as well that since she has daily aides, that should suffice, (according to their viewpoints).

Nothing could be further from the truth, as she is actually starving for the warmth of a daughter's physical show of concern.

After the conclusion of my time spent with her I realized how lucky most of us are when caring family members are frequent presences in our lives, especially in the latter part of our existences.

Therefore, indeed this was one of the saddest days of my life.

As Time Goes On

This past Sunday morning I made telephone calls to several old friends and this is what I heard.

The first one said she was about to have serious surgery.

The second one said she had just returned home from rehab.

The third one couldn't remember where *I* lived.

The next one couldn't remember where *she* lived.

And the final one was no longer living.

I'm thinking of discontinuing my telephone service.

SHE MISSED THE BOAT

I have a very nice friend who for some strange reason seems to experience unusual happenings in her life.

For instance she recently invited her daughter and son in law to accompany her on a cruise to South America. This was to be a celebration gift for her daughter's birthday. Of course the young couple eagerly accepted this lovely invitation and since they lived in New York, and my friend lives in Florida during the winter, they all agreed to meet on the boat which was scheduled to leave from Florida.

When the sailing day finally arrived, my friend (who shall be nameless for understandable reasons) got to the dock on time, only to find out that she had brought along her expired passport and therefore was not permitted to board the ship, and as she put it "I missed the boat".

"But not to worry" she thought, as there was plenty of time for her to go home to Palm Beach Gardens to get the correct passport—which she did. However on her way back to the pier calamity struck! She had a flat tire.

Again she thought "not to worry" as she had a spare which was put on the car at a friendly gas station. Therefore she blithely thought for an additional time, "not to worry".

Nevertheless calamity stuck the third time, because as she was correctly proceeding *slowly* down the Florida Turnpike, a not so kindly police office stopped her, as her new tire was the doughnut type which only entitled her to drive 40 miles per hour. Nevertheless she was issued a traffic ticket for going too *slow* in a *fast* line. All of this took up a lot of valuable driving minutes.

So sadly she really "missed the boat" as she only arrived in time to see her children waving a fond farewell from aboard the ship to my poor friend on the dock!

This Modern Age

I can't believe it—at my advanced age I seem to be a member of the younger set.

Apparently in my eagerness to contact a dead friend (I have many) I accidentally logged onto a site called "LinkedIn" having no idea what it involved, In doing so I found a whole list of people I knew and therefore checked each one out of curiosity.

Little did I know that my son (who was on the list) would send me a reply as he was anxious to find out "What the hell was going on with his mother".

After several emails from him I found out that "LinkedIn" was mostly a site used for business purposes.

Nevertheless my granddaughter Carly (she is also on the list and is my son's daughter who writes "The Skimm) was recently on a Vanity Fair clip which took place in a moving town car. So I emailed her on the LinkedIn site as follows.

I saw you on the Vanity Fair email pix which was great, but didn't your mother ever tell you to never get in a car with strangers? Carly answered me on LinkedIn "yes but she didn't say anything about limos". This was followed by several back and forth conversations with her, which resulted in her asking whether I was looking for a job. I replied that if she was hiring what was she willing to pay—she wrote back "depending on your experience". I replied "experience in what?" She then said "the workforce". I wrote back "do you mean "forced work". At that point she LinkedIn just one word "hah".

The very next moment I received a "LinkedIn" from my niece in Ohio who was pleased with my new site and explained that she was very new at this link and hoped I would please send another message in a few weeks when she would be more adept.

Incredibly another friend wrote back that she too had my message and profusely thanked me for my "link a dink".

I now believe I will be hearing from all the people whose names I checked and therefore will be unable to answer any telephone calls from regular people.

So I hope none of you will call me for the next several weeks as I'll be very busy with my new LinkedIn" friends.

Bed Solutions

Recently I was engaged in a game of canasta with 3 good friends. They are all lovely people but *strange*, and this is why I have come to that conclusion.

Somehow in between shuffling the cards and setting up the next phase of our canasta game, there was an unusual little conversation which was conducted by the three of them. I, to my comic relief was simply an innocent bystander.

One of the ladies (they really are ladies but shall be nameless) commented that a few weeks previously, she had purchased a new mattress, which had not as yet arrived. She also smugly announced that it had been purchased at a discount since one of her grandchildren was an employee of "Sleepys", a company of mattress renown, and therefore as a close relative she was entitled to a courtesy price.

The lady next to her said that she too had bought a new mattress but unfortunately at the full price. She also mentioned that it was absolutely necessary to buy it, as her old one was very lumpy and saggy and that since her late husband had departed from this world 2 years ago, she had been sleeping completely on her own side of the double head board bed that they had previously shared. Naturally the last two years had taken its toll as far as wear and tear was concerned, and therefore her side of the mattress was considerably more lumpy and saggy.

Of course it had occurred to her to switch to the mattress from his side, but even in the unlikely event of his returning to the world of the living, she did not want to possibly inconvenience him with her original side of the old lumpy and saggy mattress.

On the other hand, since his sad departure his side of the bed has been unoccupied (also sadly) therefore the new mattress purchase was deemed to be a necessity.

The third lady who was a widow as well, more or less had the same tale of woe.

She too had an old mattress containing lumps and sagginess. She also had dismissed the idea that her late husband might return and because of this she was reluctant to remove his voice from *her* telephone answering machine in order to maintain a constant reminder of his previous live condition. This message however was a bit disconcerting to her many telephone callers, as most of them were loath to explain to her that "what is dead is dead".

At any rate she too had already purchased a new mattress and had decided to sleep in the *middle* of her bed in order to leave room on either side for whomsoever might be interested in sharing.

All in all this was a very interesting way of supposedly playing canasta and I can hardly wait to do it again.

Wonderful Me

Many people have annoying habits and either do or say irritating or puzzling things that irk their friends to a very great extent.

Such people are guilty of these things quite often and generally at inconvenient times, thus causing embarrassment to everyone within their range.

It is impossible to enumerate their little quirks because what bothers some people may not annoy others.

Therefore I personally do not feel obligated to reveal my knowledge of these offenses nor the names of those of my acquaintances who are guilty of them.

However it is safe to say that there are certain social standards that are expected of everyone, and when there is an element of departure from what is considered to be the norm, then most people are entitled to be upset, including myself.

Also since I am a paragon of everything proper, I of course would never do anything immoral or unseemly therefore I wouldn't ever expect to be accused of doing so, and thus I am definitely not one of "those" people.

In conclusion I must say, I thoroughly enjoy being such a remarkably perfect individual.

My BFF

I now have a new "best friend" in Florida. I know that seems strange at this time of my life, but a fairly recent association with a neighbor has developed into an extremely relevant friendship.

She has a delightful sense of humor which greatly coincides with my own humorous view points so we have lots of fun time together.

Recently however, I unexpectedly helped her with some much needed decorating suggestions, and despite the fact that I have been a retired interior decorator designer for 7 years, I found it hard to refuse her pleas for my professional advice. Therefore I actually did perform some services for her.

I would not accept any monetary compensation as I correctly informed her that I was no longer legal but was doing everything out of friendship.

Nevertheless, after having noticed my continued usage of a nondescript and non brand name purse, she insisted upon gifting me with an extremely expensive Hermès handbag, whereupon I wisely told her that I realized there was nothing worse than "an old bag" with "an old bag", so I gladly accepted her gift.

P.S. I haven't used it yet because it was *so* expensive!

A Visit From Afar

The other day I had a lengthy visit with an old friend who now lives in a far away city. We have frequent telephone conversations which bond us together, even though I haven't actually seen her in over 10 years.

Generally our conversations contain the usual how are you, how's your family, how many grandchildren do you have now, how's the weather where you live, do you ever hear from so and so, guess who got a divorce, guess who died, guess who had her face done, guess who is no longer my friend.

This time however there was another element to our conversation because when I asked about her well being she replied "I'm okay except for my tennis elbow". I then said in an amazed manner, "I didn't know you played tennis". She, in an offended way said "actually it really comes from my osteoporosis which is why I'm in a wheelchair and can't walk, although part of that problem came about when I broke my pelvis, and besides infected toes are a handicap as well". Then she continued telling me about her pacemaker which had malfunctioned, her lengthy visits to various medical people on an almost daily basis and about all the prescriptions of supposed cure all pills she was currently ingesting.

By the time she finished lamenting about her many ailments I was thoroughly distressed and exhausted, and came to a very wise decision. I will never again ask anyone how they feel.

What News Is Fit To Print?

There was an unusual article in the New York Times that I deemed to be quite worrisome and caused me great concern, plus an amount of discomfort.

It implied that people of a certain age, particularly, those of us who have acquired the status of being "older" or even "old" are apt to be naïve enough to accept as validity, the calls from certain canny individuals who encourage us to invest in their nefarious monetary schemes, or to innocently purchase whatever they are selling.

It also inferred that our age group was inclined to be more gullible than the so called "younger set", and therefore would be prone to place trust in these devious plots.

Naturally I took umbrage against this article, as I dislike the feeling that I have been included in a group of presumable simpletons or that I am being put upon against my better judgment.

To further explain my view point, when I receive a telephone call begging me for money to aid a needy person, I'm completely sympathetic to that cause, and am generally inclined to donate money to anything seemingly worthwhile.

Does this make me an aging fool? No! It just makes me a nice person (better than most).

I do not believe that my brain is sending out warning signals to *beware* of the illegal requests from suspicious individuals as this article claimed would be beneficial to me and my age group.

In addition I think the newspaper item might be entirely correct when it implied that young people's "anterior insulars" whatever they are, light up when untrustworthy demands are made upon them, and therefore the youngsters do *not* make dubious donations.

However, since we "old codgers" receive no such signals, the article stated that we are therefore subject to being influenced by dishonest conspiracies that are made against us.

The only good thing about this article so far as I'm concerned is that the consensus of opinion was that older adults are happier and more pleasant than younger ones. (I told you I was nice), Therefore it is not such a bad thing to be so naïve after all.

How To Have Fun

I believe that the best way to have fun is learning how to laugh.

Of course everyone knows how to laugh but the most fun is achieved by knowing what to laugh *at*.

Now I would like to submit *my* list of possible laughable subjects.

1. *Fat People*—these are usually enormously obese people with huge protruding bellies, as well as other parts of their bodies that bulge out in different directions. Skinny people generally guffaw at these individuals.
2. *Skinny People*—These people often have knobby knees, droopy eyelids, scrawny necks, gaunt countenances, with sucked in chins and greatly resemble hound dogs. Fat people are inclined to titter at them.
3. *People who have clothing mishaps*—This could include drooping drawers or floppy tops and is the type of accident that is a real chuckler so long as it does not happen to you.
4. *Comedians who perform with risqué material*—these titillating routines can often produce extremely laughable reactions, however it would not be advisable

for you to laugh at them when accompanied by a first date, mother-in-law or a (possible) prim chum.
5. *Having friends who orally poke fun at other mutual friends*—It is absolutely permissible to tee hee at such remarks, but remember that these same people might say similar things about you. This is what is known as "backfiring" and is not always funny.
6. *Reading amusing articles or jokes in various periodicals, books, or newspapers* during which time it is perfectly acceptable to laugh out loud.
7. *Mutual repartée with a friend*—this is really the most fun and I heartily endorse this type of chortling as being "the best".
8. There is also an old adage that I recall hearing when I was a young child which is "laugh and grow fat—grow fat and get laughed at". Therefore it is important to know that laughter can often have consequences which may be very sad, then tears are acceptable.
9. Finally—*Side splitting laugher is not covered* by Medicare.

Attention North Pole

Dear Santa

You're my last hope. I'm Jewish but I'm what you call open minded. I'm writing to you because I need to meet a nice unmarried man and I believe you have an amply supply of them in your backpack.

Let me tell you about myself. I'm around 40-ish—Nearer to 50-ish. But whose counting ha ha! I also have had successful Botox injections—just a little (a few times).

I wear a loose size 14 and everyone says I'm "sturdy"—really strong, so I can lift heavy packages and can even move furniture.

I wish I could tell you that I've been divorced, so at least I could say I've been married—but no—I can't lie—I'm single (you know what that means).

If by any chance you know a nice man, even if he is about 70 (or more) but young at heart—please-please give him my qualifications. I'm ready to meet him any time, any place. I'll even take a taxi.

Love to Mrs. Santa and I'm waiting to hear from you before Christmas, (or Chanukah) your friend.

Ester Cohen

When I Feel Sorry For Myself

I feel very sorry for myself when I can't find something for which I've been searching and then I start thinking "what's going on here—could it be altzheimers?

I also get despondent when I'm unable to buy pickles, which are an important item on my grocery list. In fact I'm horrified to think that another person may have bought the last jar of them in Publix.

Another thing that bothers me is when the weather becomes very humid and my hair curls up where I don't want it to curl. Therefore I am most sorrowful that I have Jewish hair.

In addition I hate making dumb mistakes at the bridge table especially when the entire foursome glares at me for doing so.

This just about completes the list of my sorrowful items, but I'm particularly glad that it is not a longer list.

Relentless Dream

I must say that I am particularly annoyed by the fact that I rarely recall any of my dreams and when I do dream (which is seldom) almost immediately after awakening, the entire dream drifts away, and even though I desperately try to recall bits of it, I am unable to do so.

In fact through the years I have had only two dreams that I definitely remember.

Believe it or not I think I remember being born. I vaguely envision a dream in which there is a loud buzzing noise and everything seems to be green. Then I feel that I am a very small person sliding down towards an opening. Unfortunately after that I completely forgot the scenario.

My other dream—I distinctly recall and always enjoy relating it as I find it to be so amusing.

This is it! I dreamed that I was in a Betty Crocker bake off and I was making a custard pie. After I finished my baking process. I shaved some tootsie rolls and neatly scattered them over the pie. I then put a sign on the pie and named it my "tootsie pie". In the dream I laughed heartily and immediately woke up still laughing.

Unfortunately I didn't get to taste that pie but I believe it could really be delicious. So I'm thinking that some day I should try to dream this incident again and this time I'll try to have a slice.

Perchance To Dream

The other morning while lying in bed I started musing about the country in which I live—AMERICA and thinking how wonderful it is to be in such a harmonious place.

Everyone here gets along so well particularly in our government. The president holds sway over such a cooperative senate and congress and everyone is in agreement on every important issue, which is why the entire country continues to thrive, not like so many European and Asian countries where the citizens are always at each other's throats politically speaking and in some cases actually.

Just think of it—all the bills the president puts forth are readily passed by his enthusiastic supporters—Republicans and Democrats alike, because each person realizes that cooperation and agreement is the key to the ultimate gain for all.

This of course is why we never have dissention in Washington. Everyone there loves each other. In fact Washington is the seat of love.

I was enthralled thinking about how privileged I was to be living in such a wondrous country and what terrific opportunities are available for individual success, no matter whether you are rich or poor.

As a matter of fact we no longer have any poor people. Everyone here is equally able to live the good life—Paradise indeed!

Just then my alarm went off and I woke up!

The Perfect Solution

There is a period of time that occurs just before the Jewish holidays in the fall of the year and prior to the advent of Christmas, when many people receive numerous unwanted telephone calls on a regular basis.

These calls usually take place in the early evening when dinners are either being prepared, in the process of being eaten or just when guests are about to arrive. In other words—an inconvenient hour.

When the telephone rings, the person at the other end of the phone generally says in a very cheerful tone of voice. "Hi whatever your first name is" Are you having a nice day" And then when you suspiciously query "who is this" that person usually goes into a lengthy harangue describing the sad plight of children who live in places you never heard of, or about the disabled old people who need your financial aid right now!

Of course there are many other pleas and ploys they use in order to convince you to open your hearts and wallets wide and often, therefore it ultimately it becomes an annoying situation.

Naturally we all have our favorite charities to which we give willingly, but those frequent telephone calls from so many unknowns are not apt to encourage people to fork over additional shekels for their cause.

Therefore I have discovered the best way to defeat these financial pleaders.

When they call and begin their spiel, I then ask "what did you say? "I can't hear you" (in a very loud voice) and when they repeat themselves I keep saying "what did you say", "I can't hear you" and finally they get the obvious message. They think that I am extremely hard of hearing so they hang up in frustration. I swear this method works wonders and then it is possible for you to enjoy your dinner in peace.

Tis A Puzzlement

There is something that has always puzzled me. How is it possible to get everything out of the bottom of a jar or can?

I do have a little gadget that manages to extract olives, capers, and other solids but when there is jelly or spaghetti sauce or mayonnaise etc remaining, I just can't scoop all of it out.

I finally decided that a removable bottom lid would do the trick. Then all I would have to do is unscrew the lower end and voila! the entire contents of these bottoms would be available for use. Isn't that a brilliant idea?

Naturally I don't think manufacturers would approve of my invention, as their customers would normally be forced to buy additional amounts of these various products if they were unable to remove the residue of stuff left in jars or cans, in that case those manufacturers would gain additional revenue.

However in retrospect I also realize that extra lids would probably be an additional cost factor so the manufacturer would have an advantage either way.

And I always thought the customers was always right—oh well!

Green

I don't know how many of you people are aware that I am a vegetarian and that this is a matter of choice not of coercion.

In fact it has nothing to do with my recent knowledge that there has been an infiltration of horse meat in international cuisine. Mind you I have no beef with that situation.

It is just that when I consider the cute little frolickings of baby calves and lambs, I no longer desire to munch on their innards.

Frankly too it is mostly because I am a green person at heart. I love the color of spinach, celery, broccoli, granny smith apples, green gage plums and grass (not the kind people smoke).

I find great joy in having an all green lunch and truth be told I consume a green pickle every noon.

I never turn green with envy however, even if an occasion to do so ever arrives (and actually I prefer being a white person in my skin although this is not a racial preference).

Also I must confess that although I do love green, I am not greedy as to money. I don't care how much green money you have so long as you don't take mine (or my gold).

Confidentially I wear lot of green as well, though I am not Irish, and I definitely know when the "jig is up" which I think it is right now.

Is Anyone Calling?

To my very dear cell phone,

I am addressing you in such endearing terms simply to reassure you that I personally like you very much however I have the feeling that my affection is not being returned in kind.

You see I have great difficulty when I try to communicate with you, like when it is an emergency, such as if I am trying to receive a telephone call.

At these times I push and push and push you on your side as per instructions and *nothing* happens. You do not respond. Also when I attempt to make a telephone call myself, the same thing occurs. *Nothing*! Again I push and push and finally give up.

Therefore I would be most appreciative if you would advise me as to how we can get together when these situations arise.

After all I bought you in good faith, and while I don't wish to imply that slavery was involved (even though you are black), I was hoping that somehow we could reach an amicable arrangement whereby you would be able and willing to offer your services to me at needy times.

Buzz me at any time and hopefully I'll be able to respond.

Expectantly your most admiring owner,
Bernice Zakin

How Old Is "Old"

Generally speaking "old" is simply something that existed in the past.

It may also be an article of clothing that has been in your closet for a long period of time, or a grocery item which has an expired date.

In addition "old" can be a number of things relating to past experiences such as an old movie, or perhaps an old boyfriend. There are also "old wives tales", objects that are "old" and finally valuable (ancient) antiques.

As you can see—"old" in itself can be anything from yesteryear but the most common form of "old" is the accumulation of a person's years on earth starting from age one!

Thankfully I do not know anyone who is extremely aged, therefore the word "old" in that category is not ever used by me, particularly because I am so young.

I Am The Cookie Monster

Tragedy has recently struck my household! You see my children have threatened to sue me, even though the crime I committed occurred some 40 years ago.

Yes, I bear the burden of my past misdeeds squarely on my shoulders and willingly confess to them most humbly.

But hereby is my explanation:
I don't know how many of you are aware that the Hostess Company is probably going to declare bankruptcy (a sad event indeed). Because in their heyday of success they were the makers of Twinkies and Ding Dongs which were the main features of most young children's daily menu. But *not* in my home.

Sorry to say I was a mother who strictly adhered to the extremely rigid and healthy intake of all the food stuff my children ingested.

We only had graham crackers and social teas in our cupboard. Nary a Twinkie, Ding Dong or Devil Dog ever entered my kitchen.

Of course my children hated me (and still do) when they discovered that the mothers' of their peers graciously bought all those aforementioned tasty nonos which my children were denied.

We didn't even have Fig Newtons in my home and that certainly wasn't because I harbored a grudge against "Newt" Gingrich. Politics were the farthest thing from my mind at that time.

Subsequently when my children, Nancy and Kenny, entered their high school years they sneakily went to neighborhood grocery stores and stocked up on Twinkies etc. with their allowance money.

This was not to my knowledge however, although I did occasionally come across a dishonest cookie wrapper in their waste cans.

As I mentioned previously, I am now being sued by said children. They claim that I am responsible for the probable demise of the Hostess Company, thereby causing the loss of many jobs in that organization, and also because I ruined most of their childhoods (my children's) because of my strict observance of healthy food issues.

The cost of this lawsuit may well be considerable both to my pride and pocketbook, nevertheless, I still stand firm about graham crackers!

Fare Thee Well Sweet Things

This morning I tendered my most heart felt condolences to my daughter Nancy upon the recent demise of "Twinkies".

I know that "Twinkies" were a mainstay of her early teen years, but they were definitely not purchased by me, nor did they ever appear in my household (to my knowledge).

Actually I had secret information that they existed in an underworld sort of way, but always thought they were stashed away by an incompetent sort of mother who sneakily distributed them to innocent little kiddies, eager for verboten treats.

These kiddies immediately became addicted, and as a result they quietly advocated these "sweet things" supposed deliciousness to their many vulnerable pals. Thus Twinkies reigned supreme among a certain group of young people world wide.

Now *I* as a devoted and respectable type of parent, whole heartedly believed in preparing home baked items with occasional store bought graham crackers and social teas, as did my mother before me, therefore Twinkies would have been completely undesirable items to my way of thinking.

However I dimly recall a whispered conversation about them when my daughter was with a group of friends in my home, but there was a definite hush hush if I happened to pass by.

Nevertheless I'm truly sorry that the Hostess Company has declared their bankruptcy situation, as going out of business is always sad.

But so far as Twinkies are concerned, no doubt they will reemerge someday on another company's list of goodies, and maybe then a more modern batch of young mothers' will not consider them to be a dietary threat—as for me I still like social teas.

THE SOUNDING BOARD

Everybody at one time or another, needs a sounding board and luckily I have one, her name is Patsy, and after I write an essay or article and want an honest opinion as to its merits, I very often choose her to voice her sentiments.

Naturally I do this because like any novice type of writer, I very much have the necessity of validation.

Now Patsy, being an unbiased individual will usually pass judgment and most of the time I can rely upon what she says.

However, on the other hand, she admits to being quite flattered by the role to which I have assigned her, (chief critic) and after the many occasions upon which she has been asked to give her reaction to my literary efforts, she finally had the courage to ask me why I chose her.

With a heavy heart I had to tell the truth! "Because you're the only one here"!

FRIENDS TO THE END

The other night I had a very long and interesting dream. It was all about a recently deceased friend and we seemed to be having a great time together.

We were very busy discussing old times, what she had been doing lately, and also what I had been occupied with since we had last seen one another.

She looked extremely well and I'm not sure that I realized she was dead.

She didn't seem to be in heaven and certainly not in hell, but wherever she was, we both were able to have a nice conversation and a lovely visit.

Now I'm not about to claim that I had crossed over to her present world, nor do I think that she re-entered mine. However it was a most enjoyable get together and I am also looking forward to seeing her again—but definitely in my world!

Winning Is Everything

Guess what? I have decided to enter my name on the republican slate for President of the United Biscuit Company, as I consider myself to be one smart cookie.

Unlike Stephen Cobert—and the rest of the prexy hopefuls, I do not have a *super* pac to help me but I do have a *soup* pac namely mushroom and barley, tomato, and chicken matzo ball.

Furthermore, my monetary holdings are very meager. I have a gigantic piggy bank and if anybody out there can find the key they are welcome to open it and count my funds.

I pay lots of *taxes*. In fact I take *taxis* to various locations very often.

I am also very conservative. I only wear twin sweater sets, usually the same ones.

I definitely admit to being gay (i.e happy as a lark) and have only been married once, and am the mother of two legitimate children.

I would also gladly tell Katie Couric what magazines I read, although I read too many to enumerate. Just go to my beauty parlor and you will see the entire group of them, that are at my disposal all free of charge.

I have no hidden agendas as there is no room in my closets to hide anything.

I am completely open to anybody's opinion, as I don't even think for myself. I have employees who do that for me.

As for my party affiliations, on Mondays I can be a Democrat, an Independent on Tuesdays, a Republican on Wednesdays, and for the rest of the week, I am partial to the Tea Party—preferably if they serve English Breakfast tea and raisin bran muffins.

A vote for me is *only* a vote for me. Not for Herman Cain, Stephen Colbert, Meryl Streep or any Golden Globe personality. Betty white means nothing to me . . . I remember her when.

If elected and hired to do so, I promise to redecorate the White House very tastefully, after all, I used to be an Interior Designer and would forego my commission. I would however only serve cookies and other United Biscuit delicacies every afternoon since I believe there is no such thing as a free lunch.

With the final debate coming up so soon I'm a little worried as to which candidate will finally be selected.

Thankfully that last debate will take place in Florida where I currently reside during the winter months and that will save me travel costs.

Therefore, if I'm lucky enough to be the nominee, please vote for me at least twice. Remember I am only running for President of the United Biscuit Company so "Obama" have no fear.

A Big Event

I did it! I did it! I really didn't think I could. I got to the opening of the new Publix at 7:15AM. I almost made it at 7:00 AM, which was the actual opening time, but I didn't want to appear anxious.

7:15 AM seemed to show a little restraint and a more casual attitude, and I would therefore not seem to be so obvious in my intent to get one of the free gift bags, the first 1500 people entering the place, would receive.

Actually I was overcome with joy when I entered the premises. Everything was displayed in the most enticing manner, a real shopping paradise!

The apples glistened, the vegetables exuded crispness, the cakes and pies beckoned, and the many helpful attendants offered freebees and hints as to where to find what.

I have never been so happy since my last visit to Costco. The photographers took pictures of all the early birds including me and who knows—I thought maybe I'd make the "Shiny Sheet".

I really didn't expect to see any familiar faces, but my next door neighbor was there, Enid Pollak from my writing class was there and also on the scene were many noteworthy society individuals who were trying to be incognito and were all the while hogging the fruit and pastry counters.

The aisles are wide enough to enable friends to have conversations and not interfere with the shoppers who were eyeing the many fancy gadgets on each wall. Also, wonder of wonders every item of food displayed was super fresh.

The new Publix is like an old friend you've not seen in a long time and I think every Palm Beacher who enters the store will welcome the new premises with open arms and will definitely require open pocketbooks. These purses will be necessary as many unneeded items will be purchased.

P.S. It is now the day after the opening and my picture *is* in the "Shiny Sheet" and "Post".

I didn't even have to donate thousands of dollars to a charity event, in order to make the news. All I had to do was buy pomegranates tomatoes, potato chips and orange juice very early in the morning.

Hair Today—Gone Tomorrow

How many people are aware that America is now waging a furious war against masculine facial shaving?

Although in protest, I hear that Gillette, the foremost shaving apparatus company, has been pleading strongly for a rescinding of this phenomenon, as their entire razor blade business might go to pot as a result. (Actually "pot" itself is now legal in several states).

Nevertheless, many bar mitzvah boys have now refused to accept razors as their thirteen birthday gift items, when formerly this was the number 1 item these "little shavers" (pun—hee hee!) were looking forward to receiving, to commemorate their newly acquired manhood status. Instead they are enthusiastically welcoming these emerging wispy facial growths.

Yes Indeed! Mustaches are now a badge of honor, and beards are sprouting all over the faces of our country's male population.

Now you may ask, how did this hirsute fervor come about so suddenly? Well there is a very valid explanation which I hope to make evident in the following paragraphs.

I.e. The actual reason for this beard fervor is because many men are now becoming bald, and as a result their male ego has been thoroughly affronted.

In addition, ever since the days of Sampson, "head hair" has been a great male attribute, subsequently the loss of it sometimes causes a state of male depression.

Therefore, since so much baldness has recently occurred, a lot of men have shaved their heads completely, (which unfortunately makes them look like billiard balls).

So to prevent women from thinking that these men have lost their virility, they (the men) have grown beards just to prove that their former "head hair" has simply slipped down to their faces—thus! The abundance of beards! So America "HAIR" we come!

People I've Known And Their Attributes As Well As Their Idiosyncrasies

1. ABE ILITY
   He is a very accomplished person and quite able to do almost anything you ask him to do.
2. AL IMENTARY
   He is no relation to Ella Mentary but lives near a canal and has a huge appetite.
3. ANN OREXIA
   She's a very nervous person and is always on a diet
4. ARTHUR ITIS
   He's a real pain
5. BARBARA CUE
   This girl is really hot stuff
6. BELLA COSE
   A fighter if I ever saw one
7. BELLA DONNA
   A real pill
8. CLAIRE VOYANT
   This gal is able to read everyone's mind
9. CAL ISTHENIC
   A very athletic person—always jumping up and down

10. CORA MANDEL
    Is very stiff and has about 8 parts to her personality. She is artistic and likes to hide things—likes the silver screen.
11. DICK TATOR
    A very strong minded individual who likes to give orders to many others.
12. ELLA MENTARY
    A fundamental type—and very easy going.
13. GEORGE ATECK
    Very Scholastic and a really smart person.
14. JAY WALKER
    Never obeys the law
15. JENNIE ROSITY
    A kind giving type—really liberal
16. LOUISE IYANA
    Kind of a French type—has a definite "State" of mind, loves good food and music, speaks with an accent.
17. MARIAN ETTE
    You can always string this one along.
18. MAX IMUM
    The greatest one I ever knew
19. MINNIE SCULE
    The smallest one I ever knew
20. MINNIE STRONE
    She is always in the soup and is a vegetarian
21. MOE TIVATE
    The inspiring type
22. MORT UARY
    This guy always seems half dead
23. POLLY TICIAN
    I'd really vote for this one anytime

24. PAUL BEARER
    A real dead head always gloomy, has very few friends—not at all a live wire
25. PHIL ABUSTER
    Lives in Washington D.C. Has a lot of Republican friends, is a very talkative individual with nothing much to say and I think he wears a urinary bag.
26. SI COLOGY
    Always a helpful person, especially to friends in great need.
27. SOL ITARY
    The loneliness person I know
28. TERRY FY
    The scariest person I know
29. THEO RIZE
    The true idea man
30. UNA FORM
    This gal likes to dress like everyone else.
31. VICTOR IOUS
    He has a winning personality.

I Think I'm Right

Well here it is the next morning after the big snow, post "Sandy", and the white stuff is still here.

And since I now face a rather forlorn golf course from my 23rd floor window, I am witnessing a very strange phenomenon.

Therefore I must tell you that in addition to the 5 inches of white fluff there is something else on the ground—lots of something!

I am looking at what probably might have been trees but now appears to be the residue of an unknown Barber's shearings (not the Barber of Seville of course).

I do believe that these shearings have been shorn from the bearded faces of very elderly and orthodox Muslim and Jewish individuals, as everything is grey, grizzly and lengthy.

Now you might think that I am looking at snow covered tree tops—Not so! I am positive it is aged beard shavings!

I do hope that the shorn individuals from whom these shavings presumably emanated, have survived some place and that their beards were not removed A.D. (after death).

In any case until the snow washes away or melts, I will stick to my belief.

Packing For A Trip

Perfect advice before leaving on a vacation

1. Always bring the new night gown you've been saving for ten years, (meant for a special occasion which has never taken place) so that the person who cleans your hotel room will think that you are used to life's finer things, when she peeks into your belongings.
2. Also bring an old night gown which is more comfortable and which you really prefer wearing even though it has been mended and is slightly faded.
3. Carefully inspect your closet interior before selecting items for each day you expect to be away. Peruse carefully and make a list. Lists are very important and be sure to check off each item as it is selected.
4. If it is questionable as to which of two items should be chosen, don't think twice. Don't mull, just pack both.
5. It is also a good idea to try on any items that haven't been worn in a while to see if they fit, keep in mind that the bathroom scale isn't always wrong and you may have actually gained a few pounds.
6. If you bought something while shopping with a friend, who purchased the same article, and you will be together on this trip, be smart and confer with her to find out if she intends bringing it with her. She

may very well look better in it than you do, and then you will feel like a jerk if you both wear it at the same time.
7. Most foreign countries equip their bathrooms with luxurious face creams, and soap bars such as those from Hermes, etc. So if you are going abroad it is quite permissible to purloin these articles to place in your home bathrooms, this will impress your guests as to your chic and expensive taste. However it is therefore imperative to bring your own cheap bars of soaps and creams to use in the hotels.
8. Try to speak a few words in the language of the country you are visiting and if by some chance they answer you in their native tongue make believe you are deaf!
9. Showers are very hard to turn on in Europe (especially France) so if you are unable to turn on the water overhead and can only manipulate the faucet on the bottom of the shower wall, simply dip your toes under said faucet and use a wash cloth to launder the rest of your body. This may be difficult but saves calling the engineer who will not understand you, besides how dirty can you be?
10. If you order breakfast room service do *not* order everything you see listed, they charge.
11. Order sparingly and then maybe the dress you bought just like the one your friend owns, will fit you.
12. Have a nice trip!

I'm An Escalator

To everybody who is interested I would like to inform you that I am an escalator in a department store, and all day long I go up and down, up and down which is really a very dull life, except that it isn't a life per se because I'm not alive!

Actually I'm a thing—a mechanical device but nevertheless I'm extremely useful and accommodating even though I have a fairly monotonous existence.

Sometimes I'm quite crowded as lots of people get on me with packages, small children, canes, even strollers and walkers, and then again at times I have just a few riders, you never know. On sale days I'm busy as a bee, as most people like bargains and I lead them straight to the best ones.

However on rainy or snowy days I hate my job because I get wet and sloppy and occasionally the store managers have to shut me down until I get cleaned up.

Then too, there are people who hate me and others who are afraid of me, especially when I'm going down.

When little children are on my stairs their hands can be very sticky when they grab my railing, which I dislike intensely, as I prefer being clean and shiny.

I feel that I perform a helpful civil service as well as being convenient and time saving, therefore I should not be misused.

Years ago I had a good friend and mentor (the elevator) who actually is responsible for my existence. The elevator needed help in getting passengers to their respective floors quickly, and so they recommended me as a substitute.

At any rate I'm truly upset when careless riders have accidents while not carefully holding my rails.

If that should happen to any of you, I would suggest that I *not* be sued because I know many good lawyers who are my regular riders.

I'm Sad

I'm very sad, I hate everybody and I'm never going to stay home for an entire day again.

Everything has gone wrong—everyone has been rude and I don't want to deal with my present situation any longer.

First of all, it is now post Sandy and very few people I know have a working telephone system, so I am unable to have much wire contact with the outside world, and after you read this you will understand what happened to me.

I tried to call my automobile repair shop to no avail, as my car door on the driver's side does not open, which requires me to awkwardly climb over the central portion of the car to get to the passenger seat, then open that door (it works) and then run around to my side of the car and open the door from the outside (that door luckily works from the outside).

Apparently I now need a new lock and door handle for the driver's door side and though I know the shop has the new parts in stock, I'm not able to contact them as their telephone is out of order, therefore I don't know when I can get repaired, and I now hate the repair shop! Whew!

Secondly I tried to call my local Post Office many times and finally after 3hours, I was able to do so. I was calling them in order to obtain a premium form, which would enable me to receive all of my N.Y. mail while I am in Florida, where I intend spending the next 5 months.

The Postman who gave me that form in previous years apparently retired, and the new person said I had to get the form in person at the general Post Office.

In a very composed manner I tried to explain that since I was practically en route to Florida I was unable to come in person. He then airily suggested that I stop there on the way to the airport to get it. I patiently replied that I could not do so as I was leaving at 5 A.M. and knew the Post Office was not open at that time.

Finally I asked if I could speak to the supervisor and he said he was the supervisor. I inquired as to how long he had been employed and he said "2 weeks".

I then returned to my regular postman and asked if he could possibly get me the form. His reply was that he was not allowed to ask for it and that the general post office would have to give it to him, which of course they would not do. Additionally in a very rude manner he asked "why do you want all that junky mail anyway?

So now I hate the Postman!

Thirdly during Sandy's violence I had a considerable amount of water flooding my kitchen area from the windows in that room, which required a 30 towel mop up, and when I asked the building's (I live in a Co-op) maintenance person if he could possibly arrange to have my windows re-grouted before I leave for Florida, he replied that he would try to do so but that there were 60 people ahead of me for the same job and it was unlikely, so now I hate him!

Then to calm my nerves I decided to have lunch with one of my neighbors and ordered silver dollar pancakes in the restaurant located in my building.

They arrived (a dozen of them) without any syrup so I asked the waiter if he would kindly bring some, but he then disappeared completely and never returned to the table, thus my pancakes got colder and stiffer and ultimately I gave up.

Do you wonder why I now hate the waiter?

Togetherness

It was an extremely unpleasant day weather wise when Hurricane Sandy was almost in her death throws and thereby staying home was a necessity. However this gloomy situation did have its poignant advantages, and fortunately provided me with a nostalgic treat.

This was because I was happily cuddled up with a cup of hot tea and wrapped firmly in my leopard patterned snuggie.

During this cuddling period, and having nothing crucial to accomplish, I started browsing through an old photograph album.

I opened it randomly at a page which contained a rather unflattering picture of an unknown person who was very skinny and was wearing ugly platform shoes, plus a most ungainly and long drippy looking dress.

Right next to her was a small person identically attired in the same outfit except for the platform shoes.

I peered closely, trying to identify these people and suddenly shrieked oh my god! It was me and my daughter Nancy aged 3. This was in the days when mother daughter clothing was deemed to be fashionable.

The next page was quite similar, except in another gender. This picture was of my husband and my son. They too were wearing the same wildly unattractive printed shirts.

Then came a real disaster on the following page. My mother, my daughter and I were arrayed in the same Mexican off the shoulder blouse and my husband and son were proudly garbed in the identical Hawaiian shirts. We were all clumped closely together and grinning like we were saying "cheese". Everybody looked atrocious!

In the bygone days togetherness meant looking completely alike. But today of course my daughter wouldn't be caught dead in anything I wear and I believe I can say the same for my son and his son.

So the next time the weather man predicts a hurricane I will leave town rather than possibly be tempted to gaze at old photos.

A Letter To Someone I Hate

Actually I don't hate anyone, as I am an unusually kind, sweet person who really loves everybody I've recently met or those whom I've already known for years.

In fact I can't think of anyone who has ever irritated me to the extent of my having to hate them, as I'm truly a pollyanna type of human being.

Nevertheless if I suddenly had a personality change, and developed ill feelings possibly leading to hatred towards any individual, I might very well be inclined to write what is known as a poison pen epistle to them.

If this were to happen, then my letter might possibly read something like this.

Dear So and So,

You have no idea how much I've been irritated just by learning your name. I have definite antipathy towards you because of the vile and dreadful things you have done to me and to those I love.

Therefore I am writing this note to let you know that any good feelings I might ever have had towards you are now completely gone.

I would also demand that you erase my name from your address book and from your lips.

Here's hoping I never hear anything about me or from you again.

With as much hatred as I can manage

I am most distastefully,

Bernice Zakin

Ladies Night Out

One of the most interesting evenings a person can have, is by having dinner in a nice restaurant, and being seated at a table close to one that is occupied by 4 senior aged ladies.

These ladies for the most part will engage in what is known as "small talk" and if you are the person at the table closest to them, and will listen intently, you will be amused, well informed, fascinated, and enlightened by their conversation.

Part of their "small talk" will involve discussions about their health issues, marital views, post marital experiences (probably they are all widows), scandalous information about their best friends, or former BFF's and how much tip to leave when the dinner tab arrives.

After these ladies health issues are resolved by naming their "Best Doctors", various pains and aches, which medications are most affective, and possible curative measures that a few of them swear by, the major subject arises, "the dinner tab" which their waiter presents to the lady he deems most likely to take charge of the payment process. Now the conversation radically changes to "who ordered what", should they pay in cash, check, or credit card and will the restaurant accept 4 credit cards?

One lady usually accepts the leadership role, and if cash is the ultimate choice, then she has to collect the various amounts each person owes.

At this point all 4 ladies dig into their capacious handbags and try to figure how many 20's, 10's, 5's or single dollar bills should be given to the "boss lady. But if the decision changes and credit cards become the norm then all the cash is gathered up and hopefully returned in the proper sums to each individual.

Next, the credit cards are fished out of the wallets, into which the cash has now been put back, and the boss lady has to refigure the amount owed, including the really important item of the evening, "the tip"!

This of course becomes a lengthy conversation. Does the tip go on top of the tax or does it just go on the final sum owed? Also was the waiter really attentive, are they even going to return to this restaurant, do they want the tip to indicate that they liked their dinner, or will the waiter think they are cheap if they don't leave enough?

This whole procedure takes a great deal of time, as well as consultations with all 4 ladies, plus the annoying fact that the waiter usually hovers nearby, anxious to have these ladies leave the restaurant as soon as possible, with him as the hopeful recipient of a large tip.

Finally however, everyone at the table is content with the boss lady's decision about the tip. The credit cards are then encased in the container the waiter had patiently submitted to them, along with one pen (that has to be shared) which is used to validate the owner of the credit card, with the proper signature.

When the cards are ultimately returned to the ladies in that same container, there is usually a frantic period of "whose is whose", which person had the Visa, Master Card, or the American Express card?

Sometimes these 4 ladies forget with which card they paid as they might possibly own 2 or 3 different ones. Therefore a mix-up generally occurs and the cards frequently change hands several times before they get back to their rightful owners so that the ladies arc then able to go home.

At any rate by sitting at the table near this group, that person can enjoy a most unusual eavesdropping evening and possibly like the food as well.

Knock Knock Who's There

One night recently a loud bang resounded on my ceiling and then there was a constant pattering of feet that was obviously coming from the apartment above me. There was also a sound of scraping and dragging that was fairly continuous.

"What can be doing upstairs I wondered". The people who lived there were really old and certainly couldn't be repairing anything as they were both practically immobile and their wheelchairs didn't make those noises.

"Can it be a family of mice" I queried to myself. It sounded like it might be but what about the bang, I didn't know enough about the 'big bang theory" but maybe this was a recurrence of it.

Then again I thought it might be Venus coming down from the sky or perhaps my upstairs neighbors had been age reversed á la Benjamin Buttons.

At any rate I just kept wondering. Oh Boy! I just found out "they are moving"!

Gone Are The Dailies, etc

Do you know what is the latest popular craze? The thing that people throughout the world are now accepting as a fashion trend?

Yes! You are correct! It is the publishing of books. Whether it be self publishing, or if the writer has the proper credentials, i.e. money, social position, renown in various fields, such as motion pictures, stage roles, TV appearances, criminal fame, or even occasionally actual talent, then bona fide publishers will be happy to promote and print any written material that these people submit (with or without an agent).

Therefore we are now inundated with fat books, skinny books, hard covers and mostly soft covered volumes plus any other written material that comes under the heading of "books".

This of course is a dichotomy, as it comes at a time when there is also a curtailing of the written word in magazines, whose publishers are discontinuing the printing of various popular ones, including their national newspapers that are now smaller, thinner, less voluble and in some cases they no longer exist at all.

This is indeed a very sad situation, as ever since the ancient days of reading matter, people have been inspired and thrilled by the written word, and to think that we may no longer have the privilege of owning or borrowing these items is certainly a tremendous loss to mankind.

Of course the "Nook", "Kindle" and "Ipad", etc are presumably valid substitutes, but they do not really fulfill the needs of prolific readers.

These mechanical books that turn the pages for you do not permit you to own the actual book to put on your library shelf, and is just a poor replacement of the real thing.

So despite the deluge of new books which are primarily on the Kindle type of equipment and if you personally are a writer anxious for recognition, be content and just present your books to family and friends and simply enjoy the self satisfaction of having written them.

The People Who Are Out To "Get" You

Did you know that there are people existing in this world who are out to "get" you? They are very devious and usually sneak about doing unmentionable things to and for you, totally without provocation.

These people very often are your own children, the ones you personally cared for so diligently when they were wee tots.

Remember when you carefully held onto their tiny hands when crossing the streets? Well I have news for you, they are now reversing their roles. They have suddenly started holding *your* arms and hands when *guiding you* across streets.

This actually does not happen too often as you don't really get to see these kiddies on a frequent basis. This is because they usually refer to themselves as being "busy" whatever that means.

Nevertheless they seem to keep daily tabs on *you*. They diligently call you every morning asking the same stupid question. "How are you"? Isn't that ridiculous? They asked the same question yesterday. What do they think? That maybe you died during the night? If so you would not have answered the telephone.

There also exists another disturbing and peculiar fact that I recently became aware of from some of my friends. Many of *their* children want to take away their cars! Don't these people have their own cars? Or can't they afford to take taxis. Why do they try to purloin their parents belongings?

These same people (the children) also want to know what you intend doing with your possessions "when the time comes". Thankfully they don't mention what "time" this is. However when they *do* visit it is very noticeable that they seem to poke about in your various rooms looking intently at paintings, bibelots, etc, seemingly gauging worth.

Sometimes they question you in snide terms. "Do you really need this anymore? "Why don't you sell it and get the money? Or "it might look nice in our living room (ha ha). These are both sneaky and cheeky inquiries.

They also ask in extremely snoopy but seemingly naive terms "do you have a current will, and where do you keep it? Also have you designated your jewelry to be bequeathed to specific individuals (hopefully them). Again, have you got a vault and which bank?

These very same people whom you fed, clothed and tended to when they were down with chicken pox, measles and various other ailments have now become your best friends from afar.

They constantly refer to your idiosyncrasies when speaking to their friends (we hear about this via the grapevine in our apartment house) and also relate amusing little incidents about you (and your odd little quirks too) like the time you put your eye glasses in the refrigerator. What difference does it make where you put them as long as *you* know where they are. After all, if your glasses are near the orange juice container, you know exactly when you have to reorder the juice.

Anyway despite all these disdainful inferences we have made about the oddities and weird traits these children possess (remember they inherited many of them from you) keep in mind the fact that they *presumably* are thinking of your welfare and will most likely be just like you in their golden years!

WHAT'S WHITE ALL OVER?

I wish somebody would help me. You see, there is something wrong with my sky. It has a leak and there seems to be a big drip coming right out of it.

Yesterday it was perfectly fine. It had a nice blue color with a flicker of sunshine as well, and today a radical change has taken place.

Right now in fact it looks just like an unknown person took a large down pillow, punched it hard and then let the entire insides spill out!

Actually there is currently a whole lot of white stuff falling all over the place where my lovely blue sky used to be.

And this white stuff keeps flying around in a diagonal sort of way, as if a bunch of wind is pushing it.

And what's more, it is sticking to the ground and making everything *WHITE*!! What can it be?

Oh my god! I think it is snow!

A Happy Conclusion Is Just An Illusion

I have recently come to the very sad conclusion that it does not pay to be a good person, and I can verify that fact in the paragraphs below.

Ever since Hurricane Sandy struck so vehemently upon the shores of many states, including New Jersey and New York, I have tried to be solicitous towards many friends and acquaintances whose homes existed in these places, and no doubt were wrecked in some fashion.

I called, and recalled them eager to offer my help but nobody ever answered my calls, so obviously these people had no telephone service, or were dead, or their buildings collapsed, and they were washed away and therefore my offer went unheeded.

Then I tried to call the Red Cross to give financial aid to all of Sandy's victims. They put me on hold for 20 minutes, and then put me on automatic answering mode also for 20 minutes, but they never came back to me, and when I tried to email them, my computer claimed I had the wrong address, which was absolutely false.

By this time I was thoroughly disillusioned because I had always heard that no good deed ever fails, but then I had another disappointment. I had diligently ransacked my closets for clothing I hoped to donate to the unfortunate people who were in great need of new attire as a result of Sandy's tirade, and had made a considerable pile of items I hoped would be useful.

However when I called my concierge to find out where these articles were to be placed, no one in my building seemed to have that information.

I then called the general office, which put me on hold for another 20 minutes, and then they finally answered the phone with the sad news that they too did not know where I could bring my things.

Mind you, I had personally been called to donate these articles so I could not understand why no one seemed to have the correct information.

Needless to say I am now at a standstill. I really want to be helpful but apparently at this time it is not possible.

However, the next hurricane is due this coming Wednesday so maybe then I'll be able to try again.

The Awkward Years

Most young girls in their early teens go through what is known as the awkward stage.

This is when whatever clothing young persons put on, always seem to be too small, too large, ugly or just not suitable.

If the young lady is inclined to be obese then even the most stretchable girdle will not accommodate her curves, or to be more explicit, her bulges.

However if she is skinny and devoid of any bumps in the right places, then everything she puts on will hang miserably.

This stage unfortunately may last for a few years, during which time this young girl's self image may be decidedly poor and her parents, especially her mother will despair of ever having an attractive happy daughter.

Nevertheless time is usually a wonderful remedy and if these young persons can manage to curtail any derogatory thoughts about themselves for a considerable amount of time, then they will ultimately emerge as attractive and charming people, whose clothing finally fits!

AMEN

I am gifted! *No* I don't mean that I know how to play the piano by ear, or by any other part of my anatomy. Nor do I mean that I can emote on the stage or on the screen and then be awarded Tony's or Oscars, or even other awards for my marvelous acting abilities.

I probably should be more explicit and say that I've *been* gifted albeit in a second hand fashion.

You see my daughter has recently and most extravagantly purchased the newest IPAD, and I, as her wonderfully well deserving mother have inherited her old one.

This marvelous invention formerly in her possession is now mine. It is capable of doing the most incredible things. However, I on the other hand am not so capable.

I have to learn how to use it. I have to take lessons, make notes and spend lots of my very valuable time trying to be adept. All of which I find to be tedious, and almost impossible.

Since acquiring this wondrous item I have come to the conclusion that I am either too old or too stupid to master it.

It has so many little gadgets that a person either has to push, slide, tap or even turn, that *I* as the present owner am usually completely bewildered and befuddled when trying to get to the initial stage of its usage. Nevertheless I do have high hopes of ultimately reaching there.

Until then I shall continue reading the daily newspapers that arrive at my front door. I will read books from the library and bookstores and I will play Bridge with friends (real people). I won't "Google" but I'll "gargle" if necessary, and in general, I will continue to lead a life surrounded by the chatter of living personages and will not have to burden myself with the quietude of a mechanical device.

BARBI

My daughter-in law is a loser! Actually she is a very nice person and I love her—but on the other hand she is a positive loser, and has been ever since I've known her, which is some 31 years.

To clarify the above I must admit that what she really does is lose "things" and below is a partial list of items she has "lost" (not misplaced) over the years we've been acquainted. Any items prior to our association I cannot enumerate but according to those "in the know" many, many articles originally in her possession, no longer can be found.

Under fear of death "those in the know" will not reveal the exact amount of these items, they will merely affirm that they are *numerous!!*

However, herein is *my* list

1. Many years ago Barbi had been entrusted to deliver my next door neighbors' airline tickets to Europe (they were leaving the next day) which she had very kindly offered to pick up in New York and bring to their house, and unfortunately she "lost" them en route to delivery—this was a really bad thing!
2. According to her husband (my son) and her children she has lost approximately 20 pairs of eyeglasses

(prescription, naturally not drugstore type) *per year* since their marriage 30 years ago.
3. She has also lost about 35 cell phones in the same length of time, a few of which may have been retrieved (very few).
4. One brand new coat left in somebody's office (apparently).
5. Recently she left her business briefcase in a taxicab (not as yet returned to her, and really invaluable as Barbi is a very successful event planner, and much of her important client info was contained in a little black book within said briefcase).
6. Several sets of kcys to various friend and family abodes.

Most of the items were left in taxicabs which she frequents on a daily basis (and out of which she also leaves hurriedly, sans these items)

Many of these people closest to her are thinking of investing in a share of a taxi so that Barbi can have her own cab and can hopefully be able to recover her lost articles (as she would be the only passenger in the cab). The actual expenditure of the taxi might equate the value of these missing items.

At any rate, as I previously mentioned, Barbi is unquestionably a lovely person—but definitely a "loser".

September 7, 2013

Guess who's having a birthday
Who's reached the great big Six O

A girl who we would never suspect
As on *her* this age doesn't show

She's really a person most young at heart
In actions as well as in looks

A gal who will always help everyone
Despite what I've said in my books

She's always on hand for people in need
As her family and friends are aware

And there's no one I know who's more on the ball
A trait that's really quite rare

She's also a party planner of note
As all who know her agree

In fact if there were prizes for this
She'd probably win the grand prix

By now I am sure that everyone knows
The name of the gal we are lauding

So here's to you Barb
With all of our love
On this day it is *you* we're applauding!!

HAPPY BIRTHDAY!!

P.S. Are you finally old enough for a scarf?

Things You Never Knew About Nancy

It's no secret that Nancy was born 67 long years ago in Fort Worth Texas, also known as Cowtown. However, I doubt if there are any people still alive who remember the events leading up to her birth, plus the few years of her early childhood. I fortunately am probably the only one who still remembers.

At this time, in 1945, Forth Worth was a rather sleepy small town where prohibition still existed and there were no Bushes save one. In fact the only existing Bush was a gardenia bush in our backyard.

War was still raging in Europe and all Americans were on food stamps, plus there were shortages of everything, housing, automobiles, etc. Luckily, we had a cleaning person who lived in a trolley car and who supplied us with butter, sugar and other food items she didn't need.

We had a nice little house on the very edge of town and desperately needed transportation, and in order to get to my Obstetrician, a friend of ours used to send her 14-year-old daughter to drive me. Believe it or not licenses were available at that age in Texas.

Ultimately, we were able to obtain a small car of our own, so that we could take a trial run to the hospital and hopefully breeze there easily when Nancy was about to arrive.

At 3AM on March 1st the event seemingly was about to take place, so my mother, who was visiting in order to see her first grandchild, plus my husband and a very pregnant me all squashed into the front of our two-seater car en route to the hospital—or so we thought. Apparently we had no gas and Al frantically called a few neighbors for help. Our good friends (their name actually was Good) obliged and drove us to the hospital in their car.

We knew that Nancy was in a breech position so our doctor said his fee would be $125 for her delivery. Ordinarily he would have charged $100 for a normal birth or even as much as $150 for a C-section. Thank goodness she was born normally even tho upside down, therefore we saved $25 and actually she was the greatest bargain of my life.

The war in Europe finally ceased and then we made plans to move back to New York, and as Al's army position was at Consolidated Vultee's airplane division, we were privileged to go home in a company plane. This was Nancy's first private plane ride, a portend of her future trips. The head of the war production board Donald Nelson was on the plane and he gave her his autograph and declared her to be the best 5-month-old baby he ever saw. It was an eventful time.

Housing in New York was at a premium but again good fortune intervened and we were able to rent a lovely apartment opposite a park on Manhattan's west side. In the park I met several new mothers with their offspring and we all compared notes on our babies' progress. A $5.00 bet was made on whose baby would sprout the first tooth and Nancy won. This time she saved us $5.00

Nancy also made great developmental strides. She was paper trained at 7 ½ months so we never had soiled diapers, another saving and she spoke her first word at 11 months. The word was "paper" and she said it in the bathroom and actually pointed to the toilet tissue. From that time on her vocabulary increased everyday and at 18 months she knew every nursery rhyme. We thought she was a genius then, so I don't know what happened since.

Sadly Nancy stopped eating at age 2 and had to be fed Intravenously for a 10 day hospital stay, but again we saved a lot of money on her food during that time. As you can see—her early years were financially advantageous for us.

At 3 she became a Palm Beach celebrity and was known for her extravagant birthday parties, at which howdy Doody always performed, the full Palm Beach Hotel orchestra played and other well-known entertainers were always present. Needless to say the guest list was notable.

Along the way she met Lily Pons, Milton Berle, the singer Carol Bruce, Henry Youngman's daughter became her friend, Leslie Nielson played on the floor with her and Maurice Chevalier sang to her.

All the shopkeepers on worth Avenue knew her, which I guess some of them still do, and in general Nancy's early childhood was socially unusual and exciting.

I'm going to stop rambling here because most of you know about her intervening growing up period.

So now Nancy we all wish you the most wonderful 67th birthday and I feel particularly privileged to be your mother especially since you saved us so much money.

Nancy

"65" How can this be?

She isn't what she used to be

Back then she was a little thing

Who never thought of wearing bling

Who wouldn't eat for Pa or Ma

And never heard of foie de gras

Who went to school to learn her sums

No blackberry then to bruise her thumbs

Just Mary Janes and lace trimmed socks

Measles and the chicken pox

Then winters in Florida where she'd go

And consequently saw no snow

Poor Nancy led a sheltered life

Until the day she was a wife

First Mark when he was young and gay

And then of course he went away

Our Jeff soon came upon the scene

And from then on her life was keen

So now at last her tale is told

"But shhh!—don't tell (she's getting OLD)"!

70+30 = 100
FOR NANCY AND JEFF

How do we slice up this party?
Do we divide it in two?
Seventy plus thirty's not even
I'm sure we all know that is true

But seventy's really terrific
Especially on Jeff—It's first rate
And a thirty year marriage cannot be beat
For Nancy and Jeff—It's been great

Of course for Jeff it's been easy
Since one Nancy's not good as two
But we hope he won't make it a habit
God Forbid! He should make it a few!

But *now* we're all here to greet them
To toast them and wish them the best
Here's to Nancy—my favorite person
And *Jeff* passed "the best husband" test

So let's all *lift* up our glasses
And slowly sip with a swish
Giving *thanks* for this Minikes party
Where everything's really delish

JEFF

The first time we met him
The evening was bright
The place was at Woodmere
On a barbecue night

He arrived with 3 kids
Whom he said were all his
And they all dressed in "Sears"
Unlike And and Liz

But the kids got along
For the moment at least
'Cause they really just came
For the hamburger feast

Then Jeff stood in line
Which he swore he'd not do
And declared he would "never
Polish a shoe"

Poor Al was aghast
At Jeff's jerky air
And worried that Nancy
Might have an affair

With a guy who was married
With 3 kids as well

And feared she was damned
And would wind up in hell

But after 2 years had finally passed
Jeff got a divorce
And they married at last

After that all was great
We all loved each other
Debbie loved Lizzie
And the boys loved their brother

We truly loved Jeff
I think he loved us
We sure loved his kids
There was never a fuss

The family all bonded
They all settled down
And this group was much envied
All over town

But now here it is
It's a great time that's clear
As they've 30 years of marriage
In Jeff's 70th year

So let's wish them well
Let's all drink a toast
To the best of all couples
They're really the *"Most"!*

MY SON KENNY

65 *years* ago this month
An important event took place
No—not a hurricane
No—not a war
But a *new born* joined our human race

This kid was *really* quite large in size
Because he was born 10 days late
But thank god he *finally*
Arrived on the scene
Not *sorry* he missed his due date

As his mother of *course* I was glad he was out
As of late his size made me *wince*
However I didn't realize back *then*
That Kenny'd be late *ever since*!

Then this lad grew and *grew*
And learned how to *speak*
Although his words were quite *quaint*
He once *told me* he knew 2 very bad words
At age *4* they were "stinky" and "aint"

But at last we finally meet Kenny the man
We all know what he came to be
A husband, a dad, a golfer and friend
And he's great at these things you'll agree

Oh oh I forgot the most major thing
As a *cook* he's really a *winner*
The items he makes are truly *superb*
(If you're *lucky* he'll invite you for dinner)

So now comes the time—no more accolades
We'll wish him good luck and good health
Plus everything else his heart may desire
And maybe a smidgen of wealth!

Happy Birthday—Love Mom

Lizzie Then And Now

I remember our Lizzie
A precocious age 5
At Doral where she had her first date
When the boy (he was 6)
Arrived at the door
She hautily said "let him wait".

And when her friend's mom
Asked "Does Mark date"?
On that very long ago day
Her response at the time?
A definite "No" you see my daddy is gay!

Then soon Jeffrey Lane on a blind date with Nan
Came punctual as to the hour
And Lizzie, most anxious for Nancy to wed
Bribed Jeff with a beautiful flower

So marry they did and the Lane's joined the group
And Lizzie sure made them snicker
Thank god the siblings more or less got along
Especially when Liz fed them liquor

Soon the years passed
The kids all grew up
Three married with kids of their own

And left poor Andy and Lizzie
Bereft—two siblings alone

So she married Jeff and Mason was born
Who seemed to be Lizzie's double
Alas they divorced and Jeff left the scene
The result of their marital trouble

Never fear though for Lizzie
As Jon soon arrived
As nice as we all could wish
And now you all know that our Lizzie
Wed him and became Lizzie Tisch!

So here we all are—she's 40 years old
Let's drink to her health and the best
We all are so happy to be here
Especially since we are her guest!

JON

"The power of we" is ready today
To send good tidings to Jon
December the 7th was his natal day
And that date has already gone

But that doesn't mean "we" can't send our best
Although he's 3 days less young
And so at his clan's most ardent behest
These words will trip off my tongue

Happy Birthday to you
May *this* year be great
You're a prince and deserve our good wishes
SO even though I can*not* keep this date
I'm sending *my* love, hugs, and Kishes!

Jon At 59—2012

Happy Birthday to you Jon
We wish the best for you
It's the day that you can have your cake
And you can eat it too!

December 7, 2013—Miami

60 years ago this day
A great event took place
Joan popped a baby from her tum
And finally saw his face

This boy named Jon soon grew and grew
And then became a man
Most worthy of his family name
The well known Tisch's clan

Now Jon was not just any guy
He always led the pack
A people person at all times
Who had a friendly knack

He's friends with probably half the world
And in time he'll acquire the rest
As once he meets somebody new
H adopts them with much zest

One marriage brought him 2 great sons
But the nuptial then turned fizzy
Then 2nd time round his wife became
His one and only Lizzie

Of course then Mason joined the group
And if she had her druthers
She'd still choose Charles and Henry
To be her grown up brothers

So now this family has it all
Jon writes books and more
And his interviews with the famed
Never are a bore

Lizzie of course is always there
They really are a team
She's always fun to be with
And *sure* makes Jon's face beam

They travel the world and eat a lot
And drink a little too
And Jon donates to worthwhile things
But never forgets he's a Jew

Best of all he's now a part
Of the numerous Sterns and Lanes
He fits right in and we're proud to say
Our love for him never wanes

At last the history of this man
We've pretty much now told
So we'll just say we love you Jon
You're older but not old!

IRA

Here's to you Ira
"Hail fellow well met"
Now flying high on this
Beautiful Jet

We all got together
We don't think you knew
That this trip was well planned
Just to celebrate you

So relax and have fun
Be glad you're alive
And that you're not 80
But just Seven Five

ELAINE

There once was a gal named Elaine
And one day she got on a plane
Then moved from the east
Which she missed not the least
As the move was no loss—but a gain

So now she lives in "El Florida"
As the weather back east is much horrider
Her abode is Palm Beach
With a pool within reach
And she loves the fact that it's torrider

This lady whose e-mail name's Winiky
Would never be branded as cyniky
As she's very upbeat and really most sweet
Decidedly not at all finicky

Elaine is both smart and quite funny
With a manner that's usually sunny
So it's always a treat whenever we meet
In our class where she charges no money

But now she is having a birthday
Which hopefully will be a "mirthday"
And if I have my druthers, she'll have many others
And I hope each one is a "worthday"

Love—your prudent student
Bernice

APOLOGIES TO THE RED GUY AT A NEARBY RESTAURANT

T'was the night before friends
Invited me here
That I dined with my children
On lobster and beer

The table was filled with my
Grandkids so bright
And none of them cried
Or started to fight

They played with some puzzles
I luckily bought them
And behaved very well
Like their parents both taught them

We all ate the clams
Followed by salads
Which tickled our fancies
And warmed up our palates

Conversation flowed freely
Tho I said the least
But everyone lauded this really
Great feast

Then soon it was late
And we leaped with a start
And realized that now
Was the time to depart

So up we all rose
From our last tasty bites
And bade our farewells
And said our good nights

Holiday Blues

T'was the morning of Christmas
And I woke up at eight
With hopes that I wouldn't
Be much too late

To find that a gift
Some person had left
In a very small box
Or a big one with heft

Then I tiptoed with care
To my living room space
Where what should I see
Right in front of my face

A sofa, some chairs
And things on the wall
No sign of a gift
Not a damn thing at all

No clatter of reindeer
Up on the roof
No Dancer, no Prancer
No sound of a hoof

Alas and alack
There was nothing for me
No Hanukah bush
And no Christmas tree

This holiday sucks
No Santa—no elf
So if I want a gift
I'll just buy one myself!

Sic Sick

Domesticated animals like a cat
Or dog or bird
Rarely ever suffer from an ailment
Such as "gerd"

As they're mostly fed the finest food
Their owners usually get
To satisfy the tummys of
Each loving household pet

These energetic creatures
Who like to romp and play
Mostly all have household help
Who care for them each day

And if their owner's single
It's really is a perk
To hear a welcome tweet or bark
When coming home from work

But if you are the pet yourself
You live the best of lives
With nary any squabble
Like with husbands and/or wives!

WEINER—GET CLEANER!

I'm sad for Ex *Congressman* Weiner
Who got caught taking pixs of *his* weiner
He said t'wasn't his
And nobody's biz
Then claimed *his* was fatter not leaner

Now Weiner—a really dumb dude
Printed *pix* decidedly lewd
T'was the nail in his coffin
When he did it too often
Not just when he felt in the mood

So guys with hopes of a future
And fame in world politics
Should never *ever* print pictures
That look at all like their D—S!

What To Do!

T'was the night before voting
And my spirits were down

As I feared that my guy
Would lose in this town

The odds were against him
His future was bleak

As the polls had him losing
Week after week

The GOP lied
Bout his color and race

Tho they didn't dare do it
In front of his face

Much trouble ensued
From Mitt our guy's foe

Who claimed he'd repeal
The "Wade Versus Roe"

So what can we do?
To ensure 'Bam's the winner

Can we be a big donor?
Tho our wallets are thinner?

The answer is "vote"
It's our duty and right

Even tho it might mean
That it, takes us all night

So do it!
And make your pals do it too

Which will put 'Bam in Office *on
January Two!*

High Hopes

There's breaking news in Washington
Excitement's all around us
Will the gun *Control* Bill pass tonight
Or will it still evade us.
And will the GOPS win out
And cause the Dems despair
Or must our country lose it's hopes
And would *that* be really fair?

ELECTION SELECTION

Is 400 for a haircut now the current rate?
For a presidential candidate
Or perhaps his running mate?

Will glamour locks insure a vote?
Is Botox on the list?
Or is handsomeness the only thing
That voters can't resist!

What happened to intelligence?
Plus platforms for the poor
And is global warming just a myth
Invented by Al Gore?

We hope that this election
Will stand for items pure
The National debt? Corruption?
Or wars that still endure?

So when the final votes are cast
Our country should stand tall
By solving all these worthy things
And bring happiness to all

Let's Go Back

There is a very weird situation that now exists in America's political system.

Everything is completely upside down. Young people may start out as democrats which is a group supposedly supporting the poor and down trodden, and also includes advocates for the gays and racially put upon, as well as believers in Roe vs Wade.

Then time passes, and many elections later, when these same democrats have become more seasoned and acquire a little fame, their standards of living may improve.

They then accumulate sudden wealth, choosing friends who are more affluent and they start to travel and to acquire the luxuries of life heretofore only the republicans always seemed to enjoy.

Other changes seem to take place as well. They retire from their lovely democratic positions in government and decide to become well paid lobbyists so that sudden millions of dollars are able to pour into their American banks, or better still into their off shore accounts.

At this point they completely ignore their past democratic beliefs and abandon their former approving thoughts about homosexuals, blacks and pregnant teenagers—going politically negative as a result.

And then they join their former republican enemies and become part of the elite group on the other side of the aisle.

But how soon they forget! When hurricane Sandy occurred, the majority of republicans refused to sponsor sufficient monetary aid for the thousands of people who were left homeless, then when the tornado in Oklahoma devastated so much of that state and one sympathetic republican expressed his belief that Sandy deserved more help, the republican majority exclaimed that this man was a traitor to their party and was helping President Obama (a definite republican no no!) instead of wanting to help Oklahoma victims first.

So here we are—a divided country with no valid solution.

Will the "evil" republicans prevail and deny assistance to the poor and helpless, or will the idealistic democrats be able to further their causes.

Only time and more elections will be the deciding factors.

Attention—America

Most republicans seem to be fixated on upholding the Constitution as it was originally written, plus leaving intact the gun laws listing the original types of guns that were to be allowed.

Then why don't they also go back to the original law relating to majority rule when 51 votes were the valid number counted, and the filibuster law as it was originally written, when only one individual had to speak until he was thoroughly exhausted.

Also since the original gun law was so relevant then why can't we adhere to it, and then accept the fact that the improvements we would like to install would not negate the original enactment.

Maybe the people who signed the first copy of the constitution were really very smart, but when they enacted the original laws, they could not conceive of future generations being overwhelmed by crazies who would try to change all the carefully crafted original constitutional laws that the founding fathers stood for.

OLDER AND BOLDER

As a member of a particularly select age group (older people) I feel qualified to voice my opinion vis à vis the opposing views of Prexy Obama and Mr. Mitt, regarding Social Security and Medicare, and here it is!

I really love Medicare because it helps diminish my aches and pains without affecting my bank account and as for my Social Security check it is the only mail I get that doesn't ask *me* for money.

Prexy Obama understands this, as his mother-in-law lives with him and she probably has this coverage, thereby letting him off the hook financially, as far as her ailments are concerned.

On the other hand, Mr. Romney has a voluminous check book and apparently just one wife, so his health costs don't worry him one whit. Therefore it's no whit for Mitt!

P.S.

From here where I sit
I think that our Mitt
Would much rather quit
Than have to admit
He's now in a snit
If everyone thinks

He cares not a bit
For the poor and unfit
And regards the health fuss
Just a big load of_____!!!

Home Sweet Home

I'm moving and discarding
And my present home is really quite a mess

But with maintenance prices rising
I'm currently downsizing
Saving money is my reason—I confess

I'm selling and donating
And dumping loads into my garbage can

With possessions so abundant
(but not to be redundant)
Can all this stuff fit in one moving van?

Oh I'm tired and I'm weary
And almost at the point of great despair

For wherever I place a table
I then move it if I'm able
As I *think* it really should have been a *chair*

Also my clothes are much too many
But they cost a pretty penny

So my question's "shall I store them"
(I don't think I ever wore them)
Or maybe they'll go *on* a high up shelf

Tho I hate to stoop to hide them
They'll think I can't abide them
And to think I brought this move upon myself

Well at last my move's complete
I'm now on my new street
It's over and my old abode is empty as can be

I've performed my moving labors
And met a few new neighbors
So at last can settle down and have some tea.

SILENCE

It was extremely quiet when I entered the apartment. I couldn't hear a sound, not even the ticking of a clock, the hum of the refrigerator, or the patter of welcoming feet. In fact only the *silence* itself seemed noisy. I couldn't imagine where everyone had gone.

Here I was, home from a lengthy trip, expecting a rousing welcome and there was positively no one to greet me. There were no excited voices asking about my vacation, no arms to enfold me, no odor of a scrumptious home cooked meal awaiting my arrival.

What could have happened? Was I in the right house? Had there been an accident? Did they expect me the following day? I could not envision what had taken place.

Finally after dumping my luggage on the floor and hanging up my coat in the hall closet, I wearily sauntered into the living room, where unexpectedly 5 shrill voices yelled out "Surprise"! This was when I realized that the *silence* I originally encountered was simply make believe, and my family was truly welcoming me home.

She Was Tall, Blonde, Beautiful And Nice

Blossom Friday was a very nice girl. Actually her real name was Augusta Gormandoff, but since she had theatrical ambitions that name did not seem suitable for a successful stage career. Thus the Broadway producer who interviewed her suggested the name change.

Blossom was immediately hired for an understudy role in a major production. This was mainly because of her appearance.

She was tall, blonde and beautiful and greatly resembled the star of the show, so the understudy role for Blossom was a natural in case the real star became ill.

Of course the liklihood that this could happen was not to be expected, nevertheless Blossom diligently tried to learn the many lines required as a "just in case".

There was one major obstacle. Blossom, lovely as she appeared, was also very dumb. Not only was she unable to read in a proficient manner, she also could not remember the many words in the script.

The salary she was supposed to earn was by her standards most considerable, so Blossom decided to stick it out and hope that the star of the show would stay healthy, and therefore she (Blossom) would make a lot of money and never have to appear on stage.

Unfortunately one evening the star contracted a bad case of laryngitis and completely lost her voice.

So there was Blossom who was supposed to be ready to take on that important role. Naturally she was very nervous, and since she did not knew most of the lines too well she was just hoping for the best.

Being not too smart however, and as she was about to walk onto the stage, she heard the manager whisper "break a leg" and so she did!

"There's Someone On The Roof"

At a very Orthodox Synagogue in Brooklyn Sarah Katzoyveyavitz, a nice 17 year old Orthodox Jewish girl was going to marry a nice 20 year old very Orthodox boy Izzie Mazeltovkowsky whom she would meet for the first time one half hour before her wedding.

Sarah, who had already been mikvahed and thoroughly prepared in Orthodox rituals, in order to proceed to a high backed chair where troops of very Orthodox young men arrayed in big black hats, black coats with white strings hanging down, and wearing big black beards, marched towards her, while singing Hebrew songs and holding the arms of her very Orthodox groom. This was so he could lift the veil that covered Sarah's face so that he could peek at his bride to be, whom he had never seen. This was to reassure him that she was the real Sarah Katzoyveyavitz and not some interloper—God forbid a gentile!

When the ritual was over Sarah got off the chair and slowly walked down the aisle with her tearful parents on either side of her to the chuppah under which stood Izzie Mazeltovkowsky, her future husband. He had previously been dragged down the aisle by his tearful Orthodox parents on either side of him.

After the Rabbi mumbled some indecipherable Hebrew incantations for at least one half hour, Sarah was prodded into walking around Izzie seven times.

Finally the wedding procedure was complete. Everyone clapped madly and the young newly married couple were sent to a private room in another part of the synagogue to supposedly officially cement their relationship (i.e. have sex).

Then the party started. The very Orthodox men went to one side of the room and the very Orthodox ladies went to the other side. The room was divided by half of a Klezmer orchestra on each side. Great big green bushes separated the orchestra and the men and women,

Dancing was constant and frenzied. Men danced with other men and the women danced with brooms. The floor bounced around as they all danced kazatskies and loud wild horas. Ultimately two chairs were raised with Izzie in one and Sarah in the other, each of them holding one end of the same handkerchief. Again god forbid they should touch each other's hand in front of the guests,

Finally the ceremonies were over and everyone went home.

Ten years later a rather fat, not so beautiful Sarah and a decidely plump Izzie wearing a yarmaka were in their living room surrounded by their nine children, after eating lots of potato pancakes in celebration of Chanukah.

The nine children dutifully kissed their parents goodnight and took the Chanukah presents they received that night up to their rooms and went to bed.

Sarah and Izzie tiredly considered doing the same thing, when all of a suddenly they heard a funny noise on the roof.

Alarmed they both glanced at the fireplace from which the noise seemed to emanate.

To their dismay the Mazeltovkowskys saw a pair of black booted legs dangling down from the fireplace and then the rest of a red garbed individual dropped down into the room. The person had a long white beard, a red and white tasseled hat and a merry countenance. Santa Claus? How could it be? What would the neighbors think? Oy Vey—Finally the man spoke. "Merry Christmas" he said then he asked "do you have any cookies". The two very nice Orthodox people nearly dropped dead. They couldn't cross themselves. They were Jewish, Orthodox no less. Glatt Kosher too! All Izzie could say was Jesus Christ! The apparent Santa said "No it's just me—Santa Claus". "Jesus isn't coming yet. He's not due until the second coming".

Sarah and Izzie Mazeltovkowsky were beside themselves. They knew this situation was decidedly not Kosher but they finally came to a wise decision.

Izzie said "Santa you have put us in a terrible position. We are very nice Orthodox Jews and this is Chanukah our important yearly holiday, so would you please go back the way you came as quickly as possible".

"But before you go be sure to leave some presents for us. We have nine children and we also need gifts for our in-laws who came up from Florida especially for this holiday. So it would really be a mitzvah"

At this point Santa displayed a very shamefaced expression on his face. He then sheepishly uttered the following strange words.

Mr. & Mrs. Mazeltovkowsky I have a confession to make. I'm really a very Orthodox Jew. In fact I used to be a shamos in the Shule.

You see about 50 years ago my father-in-law (may he rest in peace) was a Rabbi who became very rich by stealing donations made to his temple, and decided to make an investment in the North pole. He actually bought the original Santa's workshop, and persuaded his very Orthodox and mostly honest son-in-law to impersonate the first Santa, who had apparently died of diabetes, as he had ingested too many cookies. So therefore I thought I would be able to atone to the world for my father-in-law's misdeeds, and in so doing I would make many people in the world happy on Christmas day.

But since I met you tonight, I've begun to realize how much I've missed gefulte fish and herring. I've longed to find Kreplach left for me instead of cookies when I come down the chimney on Christmas Eve. I'd even settle for a blintz.

However I beg of you—please don't reveal my secret and in the meantime have a happy shabos and a zeesen pesach!

Incidentally my real name is Oliver Sholem.

THE ROOM FELL QUIET AS THE DOOR OPENED AND . . . .

One snowy winter evening Marlene Simpson who was a recent widow, had been listening to a most engrossing mystery tale on her TV, when the sound on her machine suddenly went off due to the heavy snow storm. The room fell quiet as the door opened and in walked a strange man, naked as a jaybird.

Marlene was completely startled when this curious incident took place, so she shrieked loudly and was absolutely beside herself in terror.

The man too seemed very upset and tried to explain his sudden and unusual appearance.

"Please excuse me Madam" he stammered, "but I was just held up—they took my car, my clothes and my identification. I'm sorry to confront you like this but I'm freezing and your home was so close, that I had to come here for help". "Besides your door was unlocked".

At first Marlene did not believe him but when he started to cry, she felt a bit of sympathy for him and picked up a blanket which had been on her sofa, and then careful to avert her eyes so she did not have to stare at his very nude body, she threw it over to him.

Gratefully he covered himself as best he could and continued to explain why he was driving on such an awful night.

It seems, according to his story, that he had intended going to a nearby hospital to visit his brother who had suffered a very severe stroke, when out of the blue three nicely dressed young men frantically waved at his car to stop, and said they needed a lift as their car had been stolen.

He kindly opened his car door for them and was promptly hit in the head with a hammer, then they stuck a gun in his head and ordered him to undress completely and leave the car. With three against one he was unable to refuse, thus he found himself in such a dire predicament.

After hearing all of this sad tale Marlene offered to lend him some of her late husband's clothing so that he would feel more comfortable, and even made him a cup of hot tea, and applied a band aid to his bleeding scalp wound.

He then told her his name was Grover Wilson and that his wife had passed away 6 months ago.

After calling for a taxi, which thankfully arrived in a short time, Grover profusely thanked Marlene and said he'd return the clothes in a few days.

In exactly three days Grover returned the borrowed clothing and then kindly invited Marlene to have dinner with him in a grateful gesture for her kindness.

This dinner led to several more and after a few months of steady dating Grover proposed to Marlene. When she wavered in response to this sudden proposal saying it was much too soon—he said "You know Marlene, you already know so much about me, a few more months won't make a difference and that was "the naked truth"!

"Sew" Shall Ye Reap

Many years ago, right after the civil war days, Faith, a beautiful southern belle, now down on her luck was trying desperately to eke out a living by sewing and altering garments belonging to wealthy clients.

Her business was not exactly flourishing but at least she was surviving and thankfully everyone for whom she worked was extremely satisfied with her sewing talent.

One day while altering a lovely gown from prewar days, she noticed a bulge in the front of the dress, and after further investigating the gown she discovered a magnificent diamond encrusted gold locket, which apparently had been hidden during the war, for security's sake.

Faith was torn between keeping the locket or returning it to its rightful owner, but finally she realized that the honorable thing would be to give it back to her client, and she naturally expected to receive a sizeable reward.

However the client did not even thank Faith nor was any money offered to her, nevertheless she did give her another beautiful dress to alter.

Faith was devastated by this lady's lack of appreciation and decided that now was her opportunity to exact revenge.

She deliberately made the dress too tight by cutting away a good deal of the expensive fabric thereby making it impossible for her stingy client to ever be able to wear the dress.

CAROLINE

Caroline Webster was the only child of middle aged parents, who lived in a very small Ohio town, and whose livelihood depended upon the patronage of the few local townspeople who usually came to their household and dry goods store.

The items for sale were not particularly attractive but were inexpensive and therefore appealing to potential customers who had limited budgets.

Caroline was a recent 18 year old graduate of the local high school and was currently employed as the only sales person in her parent's store. She was not happy in this role and definitely had *stardust* in her eyes when she read about the glamorous shops and life in general in big cities.

Caroline constantly hoped that one day she could escape the dull existence she was forced to endure, and tried to think of ways in which she could leave her menial job working for her parents.

Most evenings she attended a nearby secretarial school and after a year's training in typing and shorthand she felt fairly qualified in her new found abilities, and believed it might be possible to apply her *clerical* skills as an honest to goodness secretary in Cleveland, which was the big city in which she had always dreamed of living.

When she approached her parents with her intentions, Caroline was met with intense disapproval. First of all her aging parents needed her support both as a daughter as well as an employee. Finally however they realized how limited her future was in their little town and they agreed to finance her trip to Cleveland and included enough money to sustain her for a 3 month trial period during which she would hopefully find employment and an *appropriate* place to live.

Off she went with high hopes and some trepidation, but unfortunately because of the slow economy that existed at the time, jobs were not easy to obtain and Caroline was still unemployed at the end of 2 months.

Then at last opportunity knocked! She applied for and actually got a real secretarial job in an insurance company where she would work for the head of the company.

Caroline was jubilant, she had already found an inexpensive kitchenette 1 bedroom apartment not far from her place of employment and she could walk to work thus saving carfare, so everything was falling into place.

She loved her job, her boss was an attractive, unmarried young man who kindly took her under his wing, and helped her "learn the ropes" so to speak.

Six months passed rapidly, Caroline was well established in her secretarial position and had received an increase in wages. Life in Cleveland was exciting and really "big town". She had made a few girl friends and was actually dating her boss Larry. All in all when she thought about her future, it was in glowing terms.

Sadly though, all good things sometimes come to an end. An emergency call from her mother related the terrible news that her father had suddenly passed away and she would have to return home immediately.

Caroline was devastated—both at the sad news about her father and that she was forced to leave her job, her friends, Cleveland, and her new beloved home. Larry kindly gave her a 2 week vacation period so that she could be of help to her mother in this distressing time.

Naturally her mother was grief stricken and unable to cope with her widowhood. Her husband had always taken charge of all their affairs and certainly it would be impossible for her to continue maintaining her little shop alone.

Caroline was distraught. How could she desert her aging mother? On the other hand, how could she relinquish her new way of life, her wonderful job and budding romance with Larry? What to do? What decision would be the right one?

Finally Caroline came to the conclusion that life must go on, and even though she was remorseful and filled with guilt, she ultimately decided to return to Cleveland.

She arranged to hire a capable sales person to work in the family store as well as a live in companion for her mother, so that Mrs. Webster would not be alone.

Then Caroline returned to Cleveland and as a "fairy tale" ending to this saga, Larry met her at the train station toting a little white ring box and a proposal of marriage.

As a final explanation Larry was definitely not "gay" so the "fairy tale" had no special meaning.

Perfect Crime

Horace Cornwell was a very simple man who lived a very simple life. Horace also had a secret. He hated his wife. Her name was Ethel and she was nasty, very dull and never smiled. Horace really couldn't stand her, and they had been married for 20 years which was a long time for him to be so unhappy with no solution, (or so he thought).

They lived in a small town in Minnesota where Horace was the only employee in the local hardware and general store, while Ethel spent her days at their home, (a little salt box type) on the far outskirts of their small town. All she did was cook and clean. Occasionally as a couple they would go to a local movie but mostly they spent their evenings listening to their T.V.—Dullsville indeed.

Since they had no children they rarely socialized. After all this was such a tiny town, where unless a person had children and could go to school functions where they would make friends with other families with kiddies, there was hardly an opportunity to be with other married couples.

The owner of the hardware store was a very nice person however, and a distant relative of Ethel's, which was how Horace originally met her. Actually there were no other single women in this town so she was his only choice, which was why the marriage had taken place.

Horace on the other hand had no relatives. His parents had died in a tragic automobile accident years ago and he had no siblings. His father had been the town's undertaker, a dour background indeed for Horace.

As time passed and as he was about 45 years old, Horace grew much more unhappy. Ethel was less talkative and they hardly had any conversational topics in common. It was a very sad way of life for both of them.

One day Horace decided that his life had to change and he contemplated a way in which this could happen.

He decided to kill Ethel. Wow! What a drastic decision. How would he be able to accomplish this terrible deed?

Finally a unique idea entered his mind. Recently there had been a raft of robberies in the area and many people had their homes ransacked, articles of even very little worth had been taken and no one had been apprehended.

Therefore Horace pretended to have a robbery in his own home and since it was a cold and bitter winter, all the roads and streets were completely iced over, plus there were huge icicles descending from the eaves of the Cornwell home.

One freezing day during this time frame Horace told his boss that he had to go to Minneapolis the next day, relating to something regarding his parents' demise, and would not return to work until 2 days later.

He told the same story to Ethel and suggested that she leave the front door open as he would not be returning home until around 3am and hated to carry his large set of keys with him.

The next morning off he went and did indeed tend to his business in Minneapolis. However he returned home around 2am wearing a heavy glove and then removed a large pointed icicle from the eave of his house.

He quietly tiptoed upstairs and using the icicle as a dagger, he viciously stabbed Ethel in the neck apparently killing her.

After that he poured a full glass of water over Ethel's neck and upper body. This glass of water was always on Ethel's nightstand in order for her to take a pill in the early morning. He also toppled the glass on its side to indicate that it was accidentally done by an assailant. This was also to camouflage the fact that the icicle was the murder weapon thus accounting for Ethel's wet clothing when the icicle melted.

He also opened all the dresser drawers and rummaged through them to hopefully convince the authorities that a robbery had taken place. Then Horace left the house and drove to the next town for a logical waiting period.

He finally returned home around 4 am, saw that the icicle had completely melted and called the police department lamenting the tragedy that had taken place in his home.

When the Sheriff arrived he did not find any murder weapon, just Ethel in her wet clothing and presumed that the assailant had taken his murderous *knife* with him so the case was closed and listed as being done by an unknown person bent on robbery.

Horace of course was then bombarded with sympathies from the local townspeople.

Two years later he moved to Florida and remarried. This time to a very attractive chatty young lady.

Luckily there usually are no icicles in Florida so the marriage had hopes of lasting a long time.

Who Am I?

I have a serious problem. I don't know for whom I should vote in the 2012 Presidential election.

You see I have lots of friends, some are poor, some are middle class, and some are quite rich.

Now each of these people are completely unaware of my financial status. Each category believes I am a member of their group. Unfortunately this is not so. The fact is I don't know where I belong.

Sometimes if I have spent too much money in recent days I feel poor. If I unexpectedly have a winning lottery ticket I suddenly enter the middle class and if by some chance I inherit a goodly sum I am rich, rich rich!

Naturally because of these frequent changes in my financial status, I attract different types of people as friends and they all seem to confide in me.

The poor ones think I am just like them and they fully expect me to vote the Democratic ticket so as to assure that all of us will be well covered medically, and that our social security will be protected.

They also think that we all have a mortgage so they are fearful that we might lose our homes or apartments if things really become dire, and particularly if the wrong person becomes president. They are really very kind people and I would hate to have them suspect that I am not quite in their category.

My good friends in the middle class are a little bit on the fence. Some of them are Independents as they believe me to be also, and we often have conversations together belittling all the present candidates and we find it difficult to make the proper decisions as to voting selections (that is if there actually is a proper decision). These people are quite intelligent and delve deeply into the political backgrounds of the candidates. They send modest sums of money for these current favorites but haven't quite made up their minds voting wise. They constantly engage me in political conversation and I must say they take up a lot of my time.

The final category, my very rich friends think falsely that I am one of them and I find myself in a predicament most of the time when they vehemently berate and defame the democrats, accusing them of *not* being Americans, *not* being honest and several other "*nots*".

They invest heavily in super pacs, and flood the mails and telephones with requests for donations to the Republicans.

They also are worried that their many millions will go down the drain and that they will hardly have enough money left to buy good jewelry, own a few residences, and heavens to Betsey, curtail their frequent travel arrangements. They complain to me all the time and send me lengthy emails predicting the Calamatous affect if the wrong guy gets into office, I really shudder to think that they will discover my duplicity as to my ultimate voting decisions, but frankly I really don't know who I am, or how I should vote or maybe if I should just move to Canada. I do have good friends there so perhaps that would be a good idea until the election is over.

Speechless In Tampa

Clint Eastwood is the former Mayor of Carmel, California, and the even more former wild western film star of Hollywood fame, who recently performed in a noteworthy manner both in the film colony and the township of Carmel, for many a moon and has just invented a brilliant new device, "a talking chair", which conversationally rose to fame in the recent Republican National Convention.

This chair not only was on stage during one of the most talked about events of the convention, it was actually a key campaign personality, completely able to voice its opinion in rather lewd and unmentionable language. Needless to say this was wholly unusual, and of course Eastwood should be commended and compensated for his invention despite the chair's rather vulgar innuendos against the Democrats.

The problem with the chair however, and I am sure time will be able to deal with this difficulty, is that the only person able to *actually hear* its words was Clint Eastwood.

Perhaps this is not necessarily a deterrent to the chair's verbal proficiency, as Clint is seemingly very well equipped to translate the 4 letter inferences the chair seemed to be mouthing.

Of course we just have Clint's word about his ability to accurately inform the general public about the chair's remarkable talent speech wise; therefore we are not absolutely positive as to its Republican preferences. So we must judge for ourselves and simply admire the chair for its presumable proficiency in expressing itself out loud, and not question its political leanings.

Who knows—it might really be a Democrat!

"God Knows" Written Just Before The Election Returns

Probably no one will believe me, but I had a strange telephone call last night from all people "God"!

Yep! He actually picked me to call, out of all the people in the United States!

Do you want to know what he had in mind? He actually wanted *me* to tell *him* how to vote. Yes he claimed he wanted to vote in our presidential election—Wow!

I then told him it was impossible to do so as his address was unknown. Heaven does not have a listed number in any telephone book, and besides no one really knows whether *he* God is a he or a she.

However I presumed he is a he and told him that even under that circumstance I could not take it upon myself to advise him, as I really wasn't sure what I wanted to do myself so far as voting is concerned.

He then said that was exactly why he chose me, as he thought the undecided were the best people to make the right decision. "You'd never be wrong if you wavered, in fact if you didn't vote at all then you *absolutely* would not make the wrong decision". (That's a direct quote from God).

At that point he claimed that I had helped him decide how to vote, based upon what I had told him about my indecision.

However he never revealed to me for whom he would vote if he were able.

Therefore when the votes are ultimately counted *"God only"* knows if the winner will be the right person.

At Last It's Over

Yea and verily, Election Day has come and GONE and most of the United States is still alive and well, although the Republican Party has a shattered complex, and simply doesn't know what went wrong, and why they lost.

They cannot accept the idea that our country could have denied Mr. Romney his hypothetical right to reign. Doesn't Mitt's money mean anything anymore? What about his nice family and beautiful wife? That should certainly have counted for something. How about his counterpart Paul Ryan who is so young and has big blue eyes as well?

Of course some folks still think the Republican loss might have had something to do with the Murdock opinion regarding God's thoughts about rape. Also that other guy's views about abortion, AKIN? (how soon we forget names) might have been a factor.

Sadly, negative, rude and derogatory comments are still being bandied about concerning President Obama's voting victory. These are Republican views of course and it is difficult for them (the GOPS) to realize that his ('Bams) presidency is valid.

Many well known people are still slandering him and among those on that defamation of character list is Donald Trump who continues to utter epithets under his breath (and on TV) regarding Obama's birthplace verification.

Mitch McConnell is equally bombastic and denies the president's right to rule, and Rush Limbaugh and Texas are thinking of seceding from the union (no great loss).

And even our darling?, ex-former non president, who is definitely not going to be in office (Mr. Romney), has switched sides again. After first wishing President Obama well on his re-election, he is now accusing him of gifting people with huge sums of money to get them to vote. He has also declared that *he* the wonderful! Mr. Romney, lost the election because of these make believe monetary gifts.

However as we all know, election times come and go and this particular one has gone the way it started, with President Obama still in office, so now we sincerely hope he will have a successful term, as America's future is our main concern.

Who Will Be The Winner?

Every 4 years America goes into a fierce competition with Hollywood, California, and produces a play called the "DeBates" with a cast consisting of approximately 8 or 9 characters.

Sometimes the play is a "mystery" as we rarely are able to figure out who is the person least guilty of political sins, until the end.

At other times it is a "tragedy" because our non favorite person seems to have the edge.

This year however, the play became a "Comedy" as each member of the cast was a comedian.

In the first act we had a Texan who couldn't remember information that high school freshmen learn in civics, 101

We also had a guy who sounded like a pseudo Nazi who kept yelling what sounded like "nein, nein, nein".

Then we had a religious zealot who uttered the most outrageous statements against women's rights.

And there was also a nutcase who wanted to send everybody to the moon.

The main character however was a Mormon who was seemingly borrowed from "the book of Mormon", the current broadway show.

The few remaining cast members were those whom we considered to be "walk-ons" and who rarely had speaking roles, and generally sat or stood on the end seats (practically off the stage).

At the end of the first act of this year's "DeBates" the hero was chosen to go up against the existing hero in Washington, D.C., i.e. our current President.

The second act consisted of a series of speeches from various people around the country who extolled the virtues and the shortcomings that existed in the two major contestants, who were in the competition for the office of the presidency.

In this particular case it was the Mormon against the present sitting Prexy, who incidentally happened to be black.

The third act usually takes place before the actual election and is simply called the "Presidential DeBates", a really big deal which keeps most United States citizens glued to their TV sets for about 2 hours on 3 nights. Thousands of pounds of popcorn are understandably consumed on these 3 nights in the US.

This year the first Presidential debate had 3 members in the cast, the Moderator, the Mormon, and the Prexy.

The Mormon was a fellow who was really hopped up on a sugar high and didn't stop talking.

The Prexy (known as the incumbent) was definitely "out to lunch", and lastly the Moderator who most likely (out of necessity) went back to his senior residence at the end of the debate.

This debate was followed by 2 others which were more or less ruled in favor of the incumbent. However at this moment we have not reached the "epilogue" (the actual election) but no doubt somebody ultimately will be declared to be the victor and at the awards ceremony the Oscar (the Prexy office approval item) will be bestowed.

When this awesome moment arrives the newly elected president (or the incumbent) will get to live in a big white house, for at least 4 years. He will have his own airplane, his own private chef, and then on his first day in office he will start campaigning for reelection. (not the incumbent of course).

Also his wife will have a whole new wardrobe and will be able to sponsor something special.

Then too he will be able to consider his future which will probably include his being able to acquire millions of dollars in speaking engagements and book deals, (not a bad future to say the least). Of course at the conclusion of this play ("The DeBates") various countries around the world will probably have registered their comments and judgments as to the merits of the play. Some of which are listed here.

The Greeks would have called it a tragedy
The French might have said it was trés trés oolala!
The Americans would maintain that it was a comedy
The English would call it a "comedy of errors"
The Germans would be insulted and say "Heil Hitler"
The Iranians simply would say it was a disgrace.

Of course there would be other supposed results of these debates in the play as well.

The gay pride people most likely would have marched in great numbers down 5th Avenue in protest against the absence of any gay candidates in the debate lineup.

Also there was probably going to be an uproar amongst African Americans, if the black Prexy was not re-elected, claiming that the race card was being played.

And certainly Big Bird would institute a lawsuit against the Morman for defamation of character.

P.S. Since it is now only October and there has to be the actual election before the final results are in, we cannot possibly predict the outcome of these invented suppositions in the play, and can only say quien sabe? And patiently wait for the end of the performance to know what actually occurs and who is elected for the next 4 years!

What To Do Now?

Where do defeated presidential candidates go to tend their wounds? Do they sit in their houses musing about "what might have been"? Do they make long blame lists and vow to retaliate against whomsoever? Is there a suitable time and place to think about possible future political positions? Wouldn't it be demeaning to accept anything beneath that special White House aura?

Do they believe that taking a course in bettering their qualifications would enhance another stab at running again next time around? Do they fight with their wives, girlfriends, children and friends? Do they still have friends? Do they buy a dog? Do their political buddies disappear? Are they now very lonesome? Do they go to psychiatrists? Is there actually a club for these people? Do they develop mental or physical disabilities? Can they pay their bills?

Do they feel embarrassed when people offer condolences to them regarding their defeat? Do they gain or lose weight? Do they listen to TV programs outlining their political errors? Do they heed them if they do listen? Do they hate the winner of the election?

Do they *despise* that winner or maybe just maybe are they really a little bit happy they didn't win so they can sleep late and not have to worry about what could possibly go wrong in the country, which would necessitate their having to make affective and correct decisions.

Only time will tell.

TRAGEDY AND TREASON

This has been one of the worst periods of time in the history of our great country.

First came the disgraceful republican refusal to vote affirmatively for a bill which would have made it mandatory for criminals and mentally disturbed people to *register* for gun purchases and to make it impossible for them to *buy* guns as well.

The irony of this bill denial was not lost when we think about the dreadful tragedy in Newton, CT that was so recent and so devastating.

After that we had the "Boston Incident" when two misguided young men set off their pressure cooker bombs, injuring and killing so many innocent people. How could this madness have occurred in our wonderful America?

In the above first incident of course, the Republicans will no doubt rue the day they acted so stupidly. Their political futures will certainly be affected, and when the next voting period takes place, they will probably find out just how the majority of voters will decide how these GOP's careers will have changed because of their dumb votes.

As for the Boston Bombers—one has already lost his life, and his youngest brother just 19 years old will either spend his future life in jail or perhaps even receive the death penalty. What a sad expectation for a young person.

This apparently bright and well educated boy had many friends in college and had participated in school affairs even in the few days after his venal actions. So what terrible influences could have motivated him to change his political ideas and attitudes towards America. He had become a citizen on September 11th just last year. Therefore it is unfathomable such radicalism could occur and cause such a rebellion towards the land that had granted him such extraordinary opportunities.

Let's hope we soon find out whether there were any other individuals involved in these bombings and also how these young men were able to obtain their explosive materials, as well as the guns they used in their killings of the Boston police.

All of this of course relates to the gun bill the GOPs refused to pass. If only they had passed it then perhaps this Boston occurrence would never have happened.

Pangs

It is now lunch time and I'm a very hungry person and really cannot rectify this sad circumstance.

Besides which I'm also a victim of the modern age as you will soon discover.

On the positive side of this situation, I have several cans of soup in my pantry closet and an equal number of tuna fish and salmon cans as well.

Unfortunately I also have a fairly empty refrigerator and thereby exists my problem.

This is it! I own two extremely modern can openers. They are most attractive, beautifully molded in elegant black, and they contain several blades and pumps that are supposed to magically and instantly open my cans, thus helping to aid in appeasing my intense hunger.

But! I don't know how to use them. They are very complicated—I mean verrry! Mind you—they are attractive but completely impossible to maneuver. I tried! Believe me I tried! But to no avail, and so I am hungry—make that starving!

If only I had a smart, mechanically capable friend nearby, things might be different, but in the meantime, I would appreciate knowing where I can find a good restaurant or at the very least, an old fashioned *tin* can opener.

To Whom It May Concern

I have a confession to make. I can't do long division, in fact I can't do fractions or short division either. Actually in spelling, the e's and a's in long words confuse me so I don't necessarily put them in the right place all the time. I either put too many or not enough of them in certain words and this applies to s's and i's as well.

You see when I was small my teachers mistakenly thought I was smart so they skipped me. In fact they skipped me 3 times so I never learned mathematical intricacies, and as you can see, spelling correctly is a challenge as well.

My knowledge of correct grammar is also very limited which again is due to the same skipping situation.

However in today's world these scholastic imperfections do not inhibit me, as I really have no need for the accurate usage of any of them. In fact to rectify the problem I have discovered a wonderful solution, which I will now explain.

I have mastered fool proof ways of managing my daily life and my method is quite simple. I mostly subtract because all items I purchase lately are so expensive that their costs always become minuses in my check book.

I only add when I weigh myself, as my scale seems to show increased numbers on a fairly frequent basis so I know that indicates a plus.

I use a computer therefore I have no problem with spelling, as strange abbreviations are always used as for instance "how R U".

And as far as grammar is concerned, I usually use prepositions to end a sentence *with* (see what I mean?)

Honestly these deficiencies do not affect me one tad, as I really don't mind being incompetent! (Most of my friends are not so smart either!)

EMAILPERSON.COM

Dear Email Person:

I received your many previous emails in which you pleaded with me to send you money in massive amounts, so that your candidate for "god knows what", can be elected.

You absolutely forgot to explain what this so called wonderful candidate can actually accomplish and how that unknown accomplishment will affect my lifestyle.

If I or any member of my family, or even among those people whom I consider to be my BFFs, accede to your request, what will be our guarantee that anything marvelous will occur for us, if your person does achieve an elected position.

For me personally, will he help to get my children into college?
(They are already graduates)
Will he help to find me a job?
(I'm retired)
Will he help to get me a mortgage?
(I own my apartment outright)

In other words, dear email person, I can't think of anything that your candidate can do that will advantageously affect *me* in any way.

Therefore I would suggest that rather than sending you money for *him*, it would be really nice if you would send some money to *me* instead, as I would certainly enjoy using said cash to visit Europe for a while.

Thank You,
(www.nobody'sfool.com)

BOY MEETS GIRL

50 years ago on a trolley car

Boy—You look pretty in that dress
Girl—Thank You
Boy—Leans over and kisses girl
Girl—Oh!
Boy—Would you like to get married?
Girl—Can we have dinner first?
Boy—What do you like?
Girl—I like pickles
Boy—I like chili
Girl—Do you have a sense of humor?
Boy—I am funny on Tuesdays
Girl—Are you neat?
Boy—No but I can change
Girl—We could get married Sunday
Boy—I'm playing golf
Girl—Okay maybe Saturday night

50 years later on a bus

Man—That's a nice dress is it new?
Woman—No
Woman—Would you like to get married?
Man—I thought we were
Woman—I mean renew our vows
Man—When?

Woman—Sunday
Man—I'm playing golf
Woman—That's not funny
Man—It's not Tuesday
Woman—That's still not funny
Man—But at least I'm neater
Woman—And I still like pickles
Man—It's getting chilly!

The woman then sighed and kisses the man on the cheek and they then both hold each other's hands and keep riding the bus.

The End

From The "Seasoning" To The "Season"

It's getting to be that time of year! Tom Turkey's luscious meat has been consumed, his bones have been dunked into several different soup concoctions and all the other leftovers have either been frozen into neat little packages, or converted into odd tetrazinni type recipes to be eaten on several nights in a row.

Yes indeed! Thanksgiving is finally over and guess what? The Christmas decorations in store windows are already in full array.

Many streets are clanging with the bells of the current season's Salvation Army's money collectors, who are hoping for donations.

Melodies of the well known Noel and Jingle Bell variety are heard on car radios, TV stations, and also from the doorways of chain and department stores.

A great number of holiday purchasers are spending all their ready cash, as well as their credit card overdrafts on unnecessary and soon to be returned gifts, that they purchased in good faith for their nearest and dearest. In fact all of the trappings of the holiday season seem to be in full fettle and are most tempting.

Even snowflakes are occasionally flopping around to authenticate this time of year, and befurred and bescarfed people rush around to get to their wherevers quickly, in order to avoid the briskness of the winter elements.

Speaking of department stores, as we did a few paragraphs ago, a few of them conduct what is considered to be a "con". They employ out of work fat gentlemen, to become fake Santas, so that indulgent mommies will bring their naïve little kiddies to sit on these Santa's capacious laps. Once there the little ones are promised the delivery on Christmas morning of everything their tiny hearts desire, completely unaware that the presumably "real Santa" is actually mommy or daddy.

Unfortunately there is a decided detriment to the Christmas festivities due to the existence of the "bah humbug" people who consider these celebrations to be bogus, and just an elaborate money making scam, therefore the holiday spirit does not apply to them.

Nevertheless to the majority of yuletide enthusiasts, it is time to say "Merry Christmas and Happy Tidings for the New Year! Although by the time anybody reads this, there may be another holiday in the offing. If so, Happy Whatever!

Who Knows?

I recently read an article that intimated Jesus Christ had been a married man.

Yes! It was an almost verifiable report that a wife had been part of his ménage. In that case many unanswered questions come to mind.

For instance if he had one, was she Jewish? Was she observant? Did he like her cooking? Had they considered having children? Did his mother like her?

Who picked out his clothes, his wife or was he his own man? After all the outfits we usually see him in did not quite have a woman's touch. A fashionista he did not seem to be.

If he was married did they visit with their neighbors? Did his wife accompany him when he made speeches? Did she get an allowance or was he cheap?

All these are legitimate queries I would sincerely like someone to answer.

And on the other side of the coin—if he did not have a wife was anyone ever trying to fix him up?

After all he was presumably Jewish and I imagine he must have had a lot of "have I got a girl for you" from various friends.

At any rate we certainly don't want to think he was gay, despite the long dress he usually wore.

So the questions remain:

1. Was he really Jewish?
2. Did he actually have a wife?
3. Could he possible have been gay?
4. Or maybe just a goy!

Jesus Christ! I wish I knew the answer!

Humor

Am I funny? That is a most difficult question to answer because I'm not exactly sure what constitutes "funny" or if it concerns me.

I do know however that I have a propensity towards twisting remarks made by other people into entirely different meanings, and in doing so I invariably use puns. Actually I'm a punaholic if there is such a word.

Now I can't really attribute my punning to being "funny" per se, although most people groan when I pun, but I don't know whether that means they are amused or annoyed.

My son recently asked me "since when have you become "funny"? However I'm not sure he is a qualified judge.

So here I am—completely at a loss as to my comedic status. Do I continue with my punning usage and quirky utterances when my friends speak or do I shut up and keep my thoughts to myself?

This is a "funny" situation—don't you think?

Rumor Has It

I recently heard a strange story. I don't know if it is entirely true, nevertheless I'm willing to believe it up to a point.

I heard that there are people out there (wherever) who are able to tap into our brains and discover everything we are currently thinking and doing.

I personally don't mind if this is true as I am completely devoid of evil thoughts and actually am a very pure minded and honest individual who never does anything wrong. I'm probably one of the very few paragon's of virtue that exist. Of course. I'm not bragging—just speaking the truth. However I realize that the majority of our many world citizens would be devastated if this supposedly great discovery was proven to be valid.

Also I think that most politicians would immediately be forced to resign their positions because once their true political thoughts were exposed revealing that they were crooks and had been pilfering from their party funds throughout their careers, plus the fact that they did not believe in their party precepts whatsoever, no one would want them to remain in office.

Then too 75% of marriages would dissolve into divorce proceedings, as wives would find out that their husbands were having affairs.

The same situation would hold true for the many husbands whose wives were equally guilty of marital misconduct.

Most business establishments would also have to close for being dishonest and probably their employees would be found to have been stealing merchandise for years as well.

Nobody in Las Vegas would play the machines any longer once it was exposed that they were fixed so the house would always win.

In fact so few business places in any country would continue to operate, as by and large most people are dishonest and would now be revealed as having this unsavory facet of their natures.

Therefore this wonderful? discovery could ruin the world and could turnout to be useless, unless of course it was discredited and proven to be just a rumor.

TSIMMIS

Who made the Tsimmis in a *pot*? The answer is nobody" because Tsimmis is supposed to be made in a *pan* in the oven, and it should contain raisins, carrots, sweet potatoes, and a little bit of this and a little bit of that, and then baked lovingly for a long time, and eaten even more lovingly on a particular Jewish holiday.

Now everybody knows this, or at least they should be aware of it, but since this piece of writing needed a beguiling title, and actually contains "a little bit of this and a little bit of that", the word "Tsimmis" became the most descriptive way to denote its contents.

Thus the title!

However the word "Tsimmis" itself can have another meaning in an ethnic sense. Let's suppose that a Jewish person wants to convey annoyance or displeasure upon hearing another person's version of an occurrence. He might then snidely say "what's the *big* Tsimmis". Naturally this type of "Tsimmis" contains no fruits or vegetables, but is merely a word defining a situation.

It isn't necessarily "Big" either, but it could possibly indicate the existence of "half baked ideas". Again it in no way resembles the edible Tsimmis which is *fully* baked.

This little narrative was intentionally written to indicate how foreign words or expressions creep into the American language and totally alters their meanings, but lends a colorful aspect to our words.

So what's "the Big Tsimmis"?

Poachers

I really love poached eggs. They are one of my favorite foods and because they are, I absolutely resent any defamation of "Poachers".

Naturally I am not referring to people who poach on other people's properties. I mean egg poachers, especially the double egg type.

There are many individuals I know who have evil minds, and when they examine perfectly usable and I might say attractive double poachers, they immediately are consumed with double entendre ideas.

I for one look at these poachers with a gourmet's eye and as a result, I only conceive of them as being useful for cooking purposes. I never think of them in terms of Sherrie's bosoms (she of TV's "The View") and certainly do not believe they relate to anyone of the male gender.

Do I have a problem or no imagination?

P.S. My husband is no longer living.

How To Choose An M.D.

Have you ever contemplated going to a new physician who might have been recommended by your wealthiest friend and found it difficult to obtain an appointment?

You probably had been told that this M.D.'s patient files was tremendous because he was listed as one of the "Best Doctors In The City" and therefore you were only able to see him because your rich friend's sister's brother-in-law's cousin's wife's uncle was the doc's ex roommate in medical school.

Naturally you were most likely completely awed when you finally passed the snob test and entered his beautifully decorated office that was decorated to the nines and which included an excellent collection of fine art.

No doubt too, it had many current fashion and travel magazines arranged in an orderly way on the top surface of an antique credenza.

His very attractive nurse could have been tastefully attired in a crisp white medical gown, and there may have been a coffee and tea machine on a nearby table so that if you availed yourself of its contents you might forget that the doc was going to be running an hour late, and judging from the 15 people waiting for him, this was understandable.

Of course when you were finally ushered into this paragon's inner sanctum you would be impressed by the many framed copies of his medical qualifications even though the schools he attended all seemed to be in southern states.

The great one would then introduce himself suavely and then examine you. He would be so skillful in his bedside (or office) manner (in which he probably majored) that you would not realize until you left his august presence, that he had not helped you a bit, but to further discuss your problem, he suggested that you make another appointment, and to be sure to please leave your check on the way out.

Therefore being completely disillusioned with "the best", your ultimate decision might be to return to your long time friendly neighborhood M.D. where there were no diplomas hanging in the walls except maybe a small one from Harvard Medical School.

There might also be a few outdated and raggedy magazines such as "Parent" and "Reader's Digest" haphazardly lying on a table that used to be in his grandmother's house, (and his nurse by the way was his wife).

However when he immediately called you into his examining room (no waiting) and after a very thorough examination, gave you his expert diagnosis, which proved to be profound, correct, and actually cured you, then you went home as a whole new person.

So who was your ultimate medical choice, the fancy one or the old timer?

If Things Were Reversed

Just suppose that everything in this world were reversed—let's say that animals were us and we were animals do you realize how strange that would be.

For instance if a hunter went out in the fall with his trusty shotgun and then came home with a trophy—How do you think that trophy's head would look on the wall? Let's see!

Just imagine your father's head hung on the wall and you—a moose were gazing at it with pride.

Then also suppose that you were a little chiawawa and were proceeding down the street watching several men and women on leashes, all urinating against fire hydrants and trees, how would you feel?

Again supposing you were looking for a pet and went to a shelter and found the perfect one in a cage—a cute little "man" looking at you with soulful eyes. Would you adopt him on the spot, take him home and then make him sleep in the garage while you "an airdale" watched television?

If these things seems incongruous to you then consider the alternative—what do these animals actually think of us?

Vertigo Or Where To Go

Generally this is the time I tend to gather my thoughts in order to face another day of complete and energetic activity.

Today I thought that if I rose early enough and then flew through my morning ablutions, breakfast, and telephone calls, etc, flying like a race horse, I would then have enough time to luxuriate for a leisurely hour listening to the usual disturbing news on MSNBC or CNN.

However even though the devastating daily news flashes were being what they usually are, I barely had enough curiosity to switch channels, or to discover what he said, and what she said, they said and what the outcome might be because my sudden vertigo attack had become very evident, and actually quite dire, so I didn't think I'd even be able to pay attention to anything that could be worse than what I was now feeling—so sad!

Our Power

Recently I was in a neurologist physician's reception room awaiting my turn to enter the great man's office.

I was accompanied by my daughter Nancy and my friend Patsy.

There were also several other people present, all of whom seemed to have no faces. This included the bowed heads of my little group as well. (Except me of course).

These heads were all intently involved in perusing their devices such as IPads and IPhones. I was the only sane person present, and oddly enough I was the one waiting to see the doctor.

There was a really interminable waiting period for my appointment during which time Nancy lost the power on her device and frantically searched the room for an electrical outlet.

At first I thought she had lost a piece of jewelry, then I realized she had lost her mind. Finally she discovered an outlet and plugged in, allowing her to once again join the bowed head group.

It was then that I had the most innovative and remarkable idea. I thought that if Nancy or even those other non headed people in the room would have their arms tattooed with the symbol of an electrical outlet, maybe they could then plug their devices right into their arms. This would mean that they would never have to seek real outlets for power.

Isn't that smart of me? It's what is known as "Power for the people".

Not Well

I'm sick—I'm a sick chick! Actually I'm not *so* sick and I'm really not a chick, but I suddenly had what is known as an "incident" akin to a bout of vertigo, which makes the room in which I am, go round and round and makes me feel extremely dizzy, nauseous and very uncomfortable.

I've had these incidents on six other occasions and I hate it! It's *awful*! Because when I experience them it is necessary to close my eyes to avoid the merry go round activity of the room, and then of course I'm unable to see anything when my eyes are closed.

Those in the know ("the docs") name this ailment as "crystals falling out of the ears". Now the fact is that my late husband had been a jeweler dealing in extremely fine gems, therefore why do I have to settle for mere crystals in my ears. Why not diamonds, rubies, emeralds etc?

Of course if these crystals were valuable gems I might willingly endure my ailment, as I could then turn those fine stones into a great amount of cash!

However this is not my situation so I have to suffer the consequences of mere crystals.

Hopefully I will recover in a few days.

MRI

Have you ever had a MRI? Well I recently had one, which I discovered to be an unusual experience, about which I will now relate.

I was actually seeking the solution to a physical problem which was puzzling me and therefore I visited a new physician. When I entered his reception room I was given a three page questionnaire to fill out which would reveal my personal medical history and thankfully I was able to write *NO* to most of the questions "did you ever have"'. Then after a short wait I was ushered into the doctor's private office.

This was a bright pleasant room filled with lovely photographs of his apparently huge and attractive family members. Some of them were attired in beautiful wedding attire and others in nice clothing suitable for additionally festive occasions.

Also on the walls were very many framed tributes attesting to his medical qualifications, graduations from famed medical schools, best doctor of certain years, etc. all of which was most comforting to me as a new patient.

When I was greeted by this nice man, he said hello and then asked me "how do you feel"? What could I say? Naturally the polite thing—"fine thank you" (ha ha)

With all the niceties out of the way we then settled down to my examination. This went well and he then suggested that I have a MRI which I was apparently able to have right on his premises. (Very convenient monetarily I thought).

I was taken into another area of this huge medical facility, and directed to a little cubby where I was told to remove my jewelry, watches, and any clothing containing metal items including zippers, and to put all these things in the tiny little wall safe that had a metal key.

I then had to encase myself in the very attractive purple paper garment that was lying on the bench. It had a belt but no pockets—so what was I supposed to do with my metal key?

The attendant who was waiting outside said "I'll take the key" (Do I trust him?) after he too asked me how I felt. I smartassed my reply by saying "if I felt better I wouldn't be here". He then responded "ha ha" 'my name is Rich. I then asked him" are you rich? He then said "if I were *rich I* wouldn't be here". Tit for tat.

Rich then accompanied me to another room (this place was enormous) where the outside wall was entirely windowed and they all had metal bars (no escape).

In the center of this mostly empty room was a gigantic machine that closely resembled an ancient Vladimir Kagan Bed. It was arranged in an angled Feng Shui position and had a series of straps.

I was then told to hop on down and not to move. I asked him what would happen if I sneezed, coughed or had an itch. He said "don't" and then tied me up. He also asked me if I wanted to hear any particular kind of music, opera, jazz, classical. I opted for show tones. He graciously complied with some "Sound of Music" melodies and then put plugs in my ears, covered me with a blanket and large eye goggles.

At last the half hour test began. I was automatically slid into the opening at the head of this so called bed and was soon bombarded with the noise of hacksaws, sledge hammers, clopping of race horse's, people banging on walls and other loud and continuous sounds somewhat like the destruction of buildings, or the roaring of trains entering subway stations. Show tunes were definitely not heard.

Finally the time elapsed and the test was over. I was removed from all the straps, goggles, and blanket and Rich kindly asked me if I heard the music. I said "absolutely no" and then he smirked and said "I thought not". It seems that the entire music thing was a hoax.

At any rate at this time I am still anxiously awaiting the results of my MRI test.

P.S. in view of what has recently occurred in the governmentally initialed IRS and the A.P. I am concerned about trusting the result of my MRI as I *initially* hoped to do.

The Elucidation Of A Lack Of Talent

My head is empty, my pen is dry, and I can't think of a single word that would help me in forming a logical sentence, or enable me to imply a clever thought.

Therefore I find it utterly impossible to write anything exciting upon an empty page.

I could perhaps speak about a series of interesting events but I am not orally adept, nor do I have a convincing manner before an audience.

I'm certainly not a mime and gesticulating is not my thing anyway.

So I am not going to continue this apologetic explanation of my inability in attempting to prove my worthiness as a wordsmith.

The End

Addendum

After the publication of this book, I may very well consider it to be the end of my writing career, so I will now bid a fond farewell to anyone who may have read any of my other books, and wishes to read this one.

Edwards Brothers Malloy
Thorofare, NJ USA
July 3, 2013